6/08

AN INSTINCTIVE SOLUTION

A Selection of Recent Titles by Roderic Jeffries

AN AIR OF MURDER *
ARCADIAN DEATH
AN ARTISTIC WAY TO GO
DEFINITELY DECEASED *
AN ENIGMATIC DISAPPEARANCE
AN INSTINCTIVE SOLUTION *
AN INTRIGUING MURDER *
MURDER DELAYED *
MURDER'S LONG MEMORY
MURDER NEEDS IMAGINATION *
RELATIVELY DANGEROUS
SEEING IS DECEIVING *
A SUNNY DISAPPEARANCE *
TOO CLEVER BY HALF

* *available from Severn House*

AN INSTINCTIVE SOLUTION

Roderic Jeffries

This first world edition published in Great Britain 2008 by
SEVERN HOUSE PUBLISHERS LTD of
9–15 High Street, Sutton, Surrey SM1 1DF.
This first world edition published in the USA 2008 by
SEVERN HOUSE PUBLISHERS INC of
595 Madison Avenue, New York, N.Y. 10022.

British Library Cataloguing in Publication Data

Jeffries, Roderic, 1926-
    An instinctive solution. - (An Inspector Alvarez mystery)
    1. Alvarez, Enrique (Fictitious character) - Fiction
    2. Police - Spain - Fiction 3. Murder - Investigation -
    Spain - Fiction 4. Detective and mystery stories
    I. Title
    823.9'14[F]

ISBN-13: 978-0-7278-6595-3 (cased)

All Severn House titles are printed on acid-free paper.

Typeset by Palimpsest Book Production Ltd.,
Grangemouth, Stirlingshire, Scotland.
Printed and bound in Great Britain by
MPG Books Ltd., Bodmin, Cornwall.

One

The house was called Ca'n Ajo because it lay in the
centre of a field which had once grown the best garlic
on the island, which meant in the world. In the master
bedroom, a woman in a pink nightdress with elaborate
lacework lay sprawled on the floor to the side of the
queen-sized bed; the wound to her temple was ugly and
blood had sprayed across the floor and on to the near
wall.

In number seventeen, Carrer Gerau Rives, Dolores stepped
through the bead curtain separating kitchen from dining/sitting
room and stared at her husband, who sat at the table, an empty
glass and a bottle in front of him. 'Is Enrique not back?' she
asked.

'Not yet,' Jaime answered.

'Perhaps I should not be surprised that he cannot be bothered to return in time to eat a meal which has taken many,
many hours to prepare. As my mother had cause frequently
to remark, man is blind to his own selfishness.'

'As a matter of fact . . .'

'What?'

'He did mention something about going down to the port
to see the Festival of the Fishermen and that he might be
a little late back.'

'And perhaps asked you to tell me, because he preferred
not to do so himself? He should have remembered that
when a man drinks, his memory takes wings.'

'I've hardly had anything.'

'By whose standards do you judge?'

She turned and went back into the kitchen where she

banged a saucepan down on the stove to express her annoyance.

Jaime used the cover of the noise to refill his glass.

The phone rang at the Policía Local station; the sergeant, who sat behind the counter, ignored it while he finished eating a last piece of coca. A man of natural authority, in his own eyes, he was not to be hurried. He wiped his mouth with the back of his hand, finally lifted the receiver. 'Policía Local.'

'So you are not all on holiday! Doctor Escarrer speaking.'

An arrogant bastard in the sergeant's eyes, a man who failed to treat him with the respect his position warranted.

'Following an emergency call, I have come to Ca'n Ajo. Señor Heron, an Englishman, phoned emergency to report he had returned home to find his wife very seriously injured. I am on duty at the health centre, so I drove to the house. The señora was dead and would have been when he phoned. I made—'

'Is there reason for us to be concerned?'

'You will allow me to finish?'

Doctors so often epitomized pompous arrogance.

'I made a brief examination of the fatal injury to her head. I have had small experience in such matters, but there's little doubt she suffered a gunshot wound.'

'Was there a gun near her?'

'None was visible. I have naturally not disturbed the scene by looking for one. That will be for you to do.'

'For the Cuerpo, Doctor.'

'If anyone needs to get in touch with me, I'll be at the health centre until eight in the morning, when I return home.' He cut the connection.

The phone awoke Dolores, who had fallen asleep while watching television. A call that late was so unusual that it must augur a crisis involving someone in the family. She might have a tongue as sharp as a butcher's knife, but her love for her family was great and where there was love, there was fear. 'The phone's ringing,' she said, her voice high.

'Then why don't you answer it?' Jaime answered.

She spoke so sharply that for once he acted quickly and hurried into the *entrada*.

She stared at the television without assimilating what was being shown. The victim was not her husband, nor Juan, or Isabel – she had made certain the children were fast asleep before the film started. But Enrique had not returned home, so he was in dire trouble. A car accident? A heart attack? A knife plunged into his stomach by someone he had been trying to arrest? 'Who is it?' she called out, her voice expressing her fear.

Jaime looked around the doorway. 'What's that?'

She repeated the question.

'A cabo at the post.'

Confirmation of her fears. 'How badly injured is he?'

'Who?'

'Enrique. Will he live?'

'What are you on about?'

She used an expression which almost shocked him. Women did not often use Mallorquin phrases of the more vulgar nature. She hurried through the doorway, grabbed the receiver from him and spoke to the caller. 'Will he live?'

'Will who live?'

When God created woman, he had used Adam's brain, not rib. 'How badly injured is Enrique?'

'He's not at home because he's been hurt?'

'I'm asking you if that is why he isn't.'

'Lady, I'm confused as to what he's not doing.'

'Then pass the phone to someone who can understand Spanish,' she snapped.

Jaime, in turn, grabbed the phone from her and hastily explained his wife became easily confused. He apologized, said Alvarez had gone down to the port to watch the Festival of the Fishermen and had not yet returned home. He apologized a second time, replaced the receiver.

'You will explain your rudeness,' Dolores ordered in icy tones.

'You can't talk to a cabo like that.'

'That I did, clearly shows I can.'

'But you know how sharp they become if you annoy them.'

'Am I not allowed to be very annoyed by having to speak to a man who is in a position of authority yet mentally deficient?' She paused. 'Perhaps I should not have been quite so direct,' she admitted. 'One should remain polite even if speaking to a Madrileño – which he must be since he is so stupid. But with the phone ringing this late . . .'

He put his arm around her. 'You scared yourself silly imagining the worst.'

She pressed herself against him, dispelling the last of her fears. Then she drew apart and said, 'Do you know how late it is?'

'No.'

'Why didn't you wake me to go to bed at a reasonable time?'

'I thought you were enjoying the film.'

'When I was asleep?'

'How was I supposed to know that?'

She stiffened. 'I suppose you thought that if I remained asleep, I wouldn't turn the telly off if there were scenes which a respectable person would not want to watch.'

Two

The smaller llaüt – the type of wooden boat with forward-tilting mast, made from four different woods and used in the Mediterranean for over 1,000 years – had escorted the larger llaüt to the west of the marina where the carved wooden figure of the Virgin had been carried ashore while the choir sang traditional songs.

Prayers of supplication had been said, asking that every fisherman who set sail in the coming year should return ashore; fishing gear and the sea had been blessed, marking the end of the festival. Alvarez turned, to make his way back to his car, and faced a young and very attractive woman, dressed in a style which was inclined to stir a man's imagination.

She smiled. 'I hope you don't mind my asking, but by any chance, do you speak English?'

'A little,' he answered.

'Then could you very briefly explain the meaning of all we've been watching?'

'Of course, but would it not be more comfortable if we walked along to one of the front cafés and I told you while we sit and enjoy their special hot chocolate?'

'That would be wonderful.'

Her enthusiasm warmed his imagination. The gods were seldom this generous to a man.

Later, after they had enjoyed three brandy-laced hot chocolates, he suggested she might like to drive into the mountains, which on a moonlit night offered a unique beauty.

She replied sadly that she wished she could, but in quarter of an hour she had to be back at the hotel where she, and others, were being picked up by a bus to be taken to the airport for their very late flight back to England.

Bad fortune never struck singly, so Alvarez had to park well away from home and walk. He unlocked the front door, stepped into the *entrada* and went through into the sitting/dining room. The table was bare. No knife, fork and plate ready for the meal which had been kept warm for him; no glass and bottle of wine to ease his sorrow.

'Enrique?' Dolores called from upstairs.

'I'm just back. What is supper?'

'A simple dish. *Pechugas de pollo Villeroy.*'

She might call that a simple dish, but in her hands, the chicken breasts in a sauce of butter, flour, cream, stock, nutmeg and pepper, became a meal to make the gods on Olympus salivate. 'Is it in the oven?'

'Is what in the oven?'

He wondered if she was bleary-minded from sleep. 'My meal.'

'Since you did not return, I assumed you were eating somewhere else and the children and Jaime said the dish was so tasty they wanted to finish it. There seemed no reason to deny them. You'll find bread and some ham in the kitchen.'

'But . . . is that all?'

'You expect me to come down at this hour and cook for you?'

'Of course not,' he answered reluctantly.

'Then there is no bother. There has been a phone call for you. A cabo, a very rude man, rang from the post to ask where you were.'

'What did he want?'

'I have no idea.'

'Didn't he say?'

'Had he done so, would I not know why he wished to speak to you? Earlier, Inés Xamerra phoned me. Since she is a woman who interests herself solely in other people's lives, you will be sure to guess why.'

'Why should I?'

'She saw you at the festival.'

'Thankfully, I didn't see her.'

'She was pleased you were so happy in the company of a young lady whom she described as dressed as a foreigner without shame. Inés wondered who she was. Naturally, I did not admit that you still leer after young foreign women half your age, and I told her you had been watching the llaüts return when a foreigner had asked you to explain what was going on. There are times when a lie is kinder than the truth.'

'That is exactly what did happen.'

'You expect me to believe that?'

Would they be dining on *gabanzos* for the next week?

Three

Alvarez approached the line of pine trees which surrounded the campo de ajo, a field once renowned and revered as far as Palma because of the garlic which grew in it. A single tooth had brought subtle taste to the poorest dish; teeth skinned, set in salt and left for months, then fried, were said to equal the pleasure a woman could provide. Learned men had met to decide why this one field should grow garlic of such exceptional quality, why garlic from this field planted in another lost its unique quality, why garlic from another field never gained it. As always, when many learned men are gathered together, they failed to reach any credible conclusion.

Disaster had struck. Quintacca, the owner, a gambler reckless even by Mallorquin standards, had lost a great deal of money and had been forced to sell the field to raise the necessary funds. To many, Quintacca had been guilty of treason.

The rough track passed through the belt of trees and the car's headlights picked out what to many was an Arcadian scene of close-cut lawns, colourful flowerbeds, oleander and lantana hedges, Judas trees, specimen cacti, and a flowing fountain. To Alvarez, and to anyone who had known the wealth of the land before, it was a desert.

He parked behind a Seat in Guardia colours and climbed out on to the gravel drive. The house, illuminated with outside lights, was large. In his present mood, he criticized the lack of symmetry, hotchpotch of roof levels, outer walls of rendered concrete blocks rather than carefully shaped rock and, no doubt, though hidden from the drive, an arched patio. A carbuncle.

Four tiled steps led up to the architectural – AKA ugly – porch. The panelled wooden door was open and he stepped into the hall. Determined to find fault, he deemed it too large – a waste of expensive space. The telephone and fax stood on a rosewood-veneered drum table (not that he identified this), which was a ridiculous looking piece of furniture. An ancient oak chair with carved date and coat of arms would no doubt be very uncomfortable. The framed square-rigger under full sail – painted by a tyro.

There was a call from upstairs. 'Who's that?'

'Inspector Alvarez, Cuerpo.'

A cabo in summer uniform came down to the half-landing. 'Carlos Nuñez . . . Didn't expect you. Someone at the post said you were on holiday.'

'Flew in from Bali half an hour ago,' said Alvarez, barely hiding his irritation. 'Where's the dead woman?'

'In one of the main bedrooms.' Nuñez was annoyed by Alvarez's abrupt attitude.

'And the husband?'

'In the sitting room.'

'Who else is in the house?'

'No one.'

'There are no staff?'

'There's staff accommodation, but no one here at the moment. The señor doesn't know why, but then he doesn't seem to be all here.'

'They must have been given the evening off.'

'Some people have all the luck.'

'But not in our job.'

The shared misfortune of having to work in the middle of the night partially dissolved their initial sense of antagonism.

'I was meant to be with a piece I met last night,' Nuñez said bitterly, descending the stairs to stand beside Alvarez.

Alvarez suffered from too much misfortune of his own to have much interest in someone else's. 'Fill me in with what's happened.'

'Doctor Escarrer examined the body and reckons she died from a gunshot wound, probably self-inflicted.'

'Suicide? Did he call the forensic doctor?'

'I did, after he had to rush back to Llueso because he's the duty doctor at the health centre.'

'Has Bopinet been roped in to take photos?'

'Not as far as I know.'

'Have you spoken to the husband?'

'Only very briefly, just to get a rough idea of things. I didn't want to cross into your territory.'

'How did you find him?'

'Almost incoherent at times and shocked. But there was no collapsing in tears, like they usually do. Odd, that.'

'English men keep their emotions to themselves.'

Nuñez sniggered. 'Not like the English women. You know the house with green shutters in Carrer José Gil?'

'I've heard of it,' Alvarez answered carefully.

'They've been threatening to close down during the summer because of the lack of trade. Too much competition from foreign women on the beaches and in the bars.'

Alvarez remembered the previous summer. Rhonda, whose midnight hair had been silk; eyes, pools of mocking temptation; lips velvet allures. He pulled his thoughts back to order. 'Like to lead the way to the bedroom?'

They went up the stairs, which divided at the half-landing, and went along a wide corridor and into the end room. The many overhead lights were on, illuminating the largest bedroom Alvarez had ever seen – more like a furnished ballroom. The emperor-sized bed was overlaid with a beautifully embroidered throw; the curtains were draped; there was an elaborately inlaid dressing table with cross-over feet, on which stood two glasses and above which hung an oval gilt-wood mirror. There were a pair of carved oak side chairs; a small bookcase cupboard filled with leather-bound books; two matching Aubusson rugs; and a painting by a local artist who had gained an international reputation. A split air-conditioning unit provided cool in summer, heat in winter. Money might not buy happiness, but it secured comfort.

Alvarez reluctantly studied the dead woman, huddled across the tiled floor and a corner of one of the rugs. The circular wound in her right temple shocked; there was a thin, dark, broken ring around it. Disturbingly, about her closed lips was the suggestion of a smile, not the grimace of death – a phenomenon he had noted before.

He looked away from her. The curtains had been carefully drawn across closed windows – odd until one realized that the air conditioning would deliver whatever temperature one wanted. The bed covers were uncreased, the rugs were squarely in place, despite her lying partially across one. The only visible signs of untidiness were the flute and tumbler on the dressing table, a bottle of champagne in a chilling sleeve on the floor by the side of the dressing table, and the blood splattering.

'Have you searched the room?' he asked.

'Not touched a thing.'

'You'll have noticed there's no gun?'

'I reckoned she must have let go of it as she fell and it skidded under something; maybe the bed.'

Yet that seemed unlikely, considering the position in which she had probably been standing meant the gun would have fallen on a rug, not the tiled floor. But experience showed it was dangerous to dismiss the unlikely. 'Another thing I don't see is a note.'

'Why d'you expect to?'

'There's normally one explaining either why the person's committing suicide or trying to justify the action.'

A visual search of the bedroom uncovered no gun or suicide note; neither was either in the dressing room or bathroom.

Alvarez stood in the middle of the bedroom. Whatever Doctor Escarrer had said, the lack of a gun spelled murder – a conclusion reinforced by the further lack of a suicide note.

There was a call from below. He spoke to Nuñez. 'That's likely the forensic doctor – would you like to go down and bring him up here?'

Nuñez did not like, but did as asked.

Superior Chief Salas often bored his listener by repeating a precept more than thrice, and one of the things he often bored Alvarez with was that in every criminal investigation, one of the most important things to do was to note if anything appeared out of character. The two glasses. It was odd that in a house where antique furniture appeared to be treasured, two glasses should have been left on what was probably a valuable dressing table, since they might so readily mark the wood; and why had the bottle of champagne been left on the floor?

There was a brief murmur of voices before Doctor Noguero, followed by Nuñez, entered.

Noguero – short, thin, casually dressed with a hint of style – came forward and shook hands. 'Pleasure to meet you again, Inspector, even if we only seem to do so in the company of tragedy.' He put down on the floor the battered leather case he had been carrying in his left hand.

He crossed the room to stand close to the dead woman, visually studied her for a while before he said 'What can you tell me?'

'Very little, I'm afraid,' Alvarez answered. 'I didn't arrive until Doctor Escarrer had left, but I understand he suggested it was death by gunshot and the probability of suicide.'

'That broken, dark ring about the wound shows the dirty muzzle of a pistol was placed against the skin before it was fired . . . Who found her?'

'The husband.'

Noguero began a slow, careful examination of the body without moving it, but displacing clothes where necessary. Alvarez stared out through the nearer window. Presumably, the dead were beyond embarrassment at the invasion of their bodies; but embarrassment could still be suffered by those who were present.

Noguero stood upright and arched his back to ease it. 'Rigor has not yet appeared and together with the temperature of the body this suggests death occurred roughly three to four hours ago. As always, that is only an estimate, but perhaps, despite the high air temperatures, a little more reliable than usual since death was a relatively short time ago.

'The wound to the temple – a common site of election – is split, scorched, slightly blackened and there are particles of burned powder. It was a contact wound.'

'Suicide is confirmed?'

' I imagine Doctor Escarrer restricted himself to making certain she was dead and did not examine the rest of the body?'

'I'll call the cabo who was here to find out.'

'No need for that. If he had found the second wound, he would have reported it.'

'A second one?'

'Another gunshot wound to the thigh. This became apparent when I moved the body on to the other side. Her clothing must be sent to the laboratory and tested for residue, but I doubt any will be found. I'm reasonably certain the shot was fired from a distance.'

'Then that and the missing gun talk murder,' Alvarez said glumly. A prolonged investigation was going to have to be carried out.

'It seems so.'

'Why the shot to the thigh as well as the head?' He was speaking to himself as much as to the other.

Noguero pulled off his surgical gloves, brought a plastic bag out of his case and dropped the gloves into this. 'If one accepts that the shot was fired from a distance – say ten, twelve feet – then I can only think of two possibilities. The first shot was aimed at the heart, but the murderer had little experience of handguns. It has often been said that, in such circumstances, the safest place to be is in front of the gun. Or it was a case of nerves, not incompetence. A man can be a good shot at a target, yet when it comes to kill in cold blood, his hand shakes.

'The bullet in the thigh would have brought her crashing down, in great pain, almost certainly screaming. The murderer needed to quieten her and made certain the second shot was fatal by pressing the muzzle against her head.'

'What a way to go!'

'Death is seldom pleasant.'

Doctors were so openly pessimistic.

'You can have the body moved to the morgue. I'll carry out the post-mortem as soon as possible.'

Alvarez accompanied Noguero downstairs, watched him

drive away. He crossed to the phone on the table under the mirror, gained perverse pleasure from knowing he would be interrupting both the undertaker's and Bopinet's sleep.

He returned upstairs to the bedroom, crossed to the two glasses on the dressing table. In the bottom of the flute was a very small amount of champagne. The second glass was almost dry, but it smelled of whisky. There had been two drinkers.

Bopinet was much taller and more slightly built than the average Mallorquin; remembering Claudio Bopinet had been short and plump, there were those who wondered who his true father had been.

'Why the hell does this sort of thing always happen in the middle of the night?' he asked bad-temperedly, as he stepped into Ca'n Ajo and put his photographic equipment down on the floor.

'We live in an unkind world,' Alvarez answered.

'Bloody crazy. My next door neighbour is a pig of a man, yet last week he won a fortune on a decimo.'

'Perhaps he'll spend it all quickly and stupidly.'

'When he makes a miser appear generous? Not even an offer of a drink to celebrate. Where's the victim?'

'In one of the main bedrooms.'

'Would you like to carry that bag and save my shoulder?'

Always eager to share his burden, Alvarez thought sourly. He picked up a heavy leather case with a long carrying strap.

They climbed the stairs, entered the bedroom. After dropping the small bag he had been carrying, Bopinet stepped forward and stared down at the dead woman. 'Her head's in a bit of a mess.'

Alvarez could not understand how anyone, however experienced, could so casually accept the evidence of violent death.

'What are the orders? Broad shots all round, close-ups of the wound?'

About to say wounds, Alvarez checked the word. To photograph the wound to her thigh meant disturbing her nightdress and because of his sense of embarrassment, he was reluctant for that to be done. The wound had not been visible until she was moved, so nothing would be lost by waiting to photograph it until she was in the morgue and he would, hopefully, escape his duty of being there. 'As you say. In addition, get a close-up of the two glasses and the bottle of champagne in the cooler.'

Bopinet took three shots of the wound, passed the digital camera to Alvarez. 'Is that how you want it?'

Photography could insulate the viewer from the horror of what he was looking at, but Alvarez again inwardly shuddered as he stared at the image of the savage wound to the woman's head, and thought longingly of a cool glass of brandy followed by oblivion and his bed.

Four

In the sitting room – large, furnished with modern and antique furniture which managed to complement each other, not offend – Nuñez sat and watched television on a very large, flat screen. Señor Heron, the husband of the deceased, in another of the four armchairs, stared into space. He showed no interest in Alvarez's arrival.

'Señor Heron, I am Inspector Alvarez of the Cuerpo General de Policia,' he said in English. 'I should like to say how very much I regret this tragedy.'

Heron looked briefly at him, then away.

Close to middle age, Alvarez judged, but not yet touched by the disadvantages to come; his hair had not begun to retreat; the flesh on his face was taut and almost unlined; even seated, it was obvious his body was in good shape.

'I fear I must ask you a few questions. I will be brief, but there are certain facts I need to know.'

Heron gripped the arms of the chair.

'Will you tell me what happened from the time you arrived back here.'

'Oh, Christ!' he mumbled. 'I . . . I need a drink.'

'What would you like and where will we find it?'

Heron pointed across the room at a door.

'See what's there, will you?' Alvarez said to the cabo.

To their surprise, the door opened on to a small bar – shelves with a range of bottles which were multiplied by the wall mirror; oak bar; stools; and a mirror advert, in colour, for Pastis.

'What would you like us to get you?' Alvarez asked for the second time.

Heron gave no answer.

'Brandy, gin, whisky?'

Finally, he answered, 'Whisky.'

'With soda and ice?'

'No.'

Alvarez spoke to Nuñez. 'Pour a strong one.'

Nuñez, who had been studying the bottles, turned. 'There are half a dozen makes of whisky.'

'Choose the nearest.'

He bent down and opened a cupboard below the bar, brought out three glasses, set them down. 'Thought one wouldn't do us any harm.'

Hardly a time for them to enjoy a drink, Alvarez judged. But perhaps it would seem more normal for Heron if they did not leave him to drink on his own. 'For me, the same with some ice.'

Heron's hands shook so much, he had to hold the glass with both; when he raised it to his mouth, it tapped his teeth loudly enough to be heard.

Alvarez drank. Even though he had seldom had the chance to enjoy it, he could recognize a good malt whisky. Liquid velvet . . .

Heron dropped his glass to the carpet. It did not break and only a few drops of liquid and three-quarters melted ice cubes spilled out. Alvarez crossed the floor to scoop up the ice into the glass. 'I'll refill it, señor.'

Heron might not have heard.

'You can do the same for me,' Nuñez said.

Alvarez ignored the request, walked over to the bar, refilled the one glass. He handed this to Heron, returned to his seat. 'Señor, I understand from my colleague that you told him you drove back here shortly before you made the tragic discovery. Where had you been?'

'I don't remember,' he answered wildly.

'You had been with friends?'

'I tell you, I can't remember.'

'Then we'll move on. What did you do after arriving back here?'

Heron's seething emotions were reflected by the lines on his face. What memories was he suffering? Alvarez wondered. To watch raw emotion could be almost as painful as suffering it.

'I came inside . . .' He stopped.

'Was the front door locked?'

'No.'

'That must have surprised you?'

'I thought we'd been burgled again.'

'Again?'

'We lost all the digital equipment and a few pieces of silver.'

'When was this?'

'At the end of May.'

'Was the thief arrested?'

Heron rubbed his forehead. 'They said they knew who he was, but there wasn't enough evidence.'

'Thinking you had been burgled, what did you do next?'

'Searched downstairs and then . . . went up and . . .'

'You found, most tragically, that your wife was dead. You phoned Emergency. Did you use the phone from the bedroom?'

'Yes.'

'Was there a handwritten note by the phone?'

'No.'

'Did you find such a note anywhere else?'

He shook his head.

'Was there a gun by the side of your wife?'

'No.'

'You can be certain of that?'

'Do you think the image of what I saw isn't burned into my brain?' he asked wildly.

'Señor, this has to be so distressing for you that I will be brief. Can you say at what time you returned home?'

'It was latish.' Heron spoke more calmly.

'You cannot be more accurate?'

'No.'

'Did you phone 112, Emergency, as soon as you found your wife in the bedroom?'

'Yes.'

'The call will have been logged so we will be able to note the time.'

'What the hell's that matter?'

'We have to be as precise as possible, señor.'

'I'm . . . I'm sorry.'

'There is no need whatsoever to apologize. In the circumstances, you are helping us a great deal. Can you yet
remember where you had been before you returned?'

'Down in the port.'

'Doing what?'

'Having a drink at one of the front cafés.'

'Were you on your own?'

'Yes.'

'While down there, did you see anyone you knew?'

'No.'

Alvarez knew how difficult it would be to confirm such
an alibi on a night as busy as the Festival of the Fishermen,
and sighed inwardly.

'Does your wife—' He checked his words. The present
was no longer apposite; the past was cruel. 'Is there much
jewellery in the house?'

'Quite a lot.'

'Did you make certain none of it was missing?'

'No.'

'Not when you had reason to think there may have been
another burglary?'

'It's in the safe in her bedroom. When I went in . . . saw
her lying there . . .'

'Of course. But it is important to know if her safe had
been burgled. Perhaps you will be kind enough to check?'

'I can't.'

'Señor, I'm afraid you must.'

'I don't know where the key is.'

Initially, Alvarez thought Heron was too shocked to understand what he was saying. 'Why is that?'

'She . . .'

He waited.

'She liked to control her own affairs.'

'Will you permit me to search for the key?'

'Yes.'

'Thank you. And when I find it, I must ask you to check
the jewellery.'

He left, went upstairs and into the dead woman's bedroom. He searched where keys were usually hidden – on the dressing table, in the bedside cabinet, in the drawer of expensive silk underwear in the dressing room – and to his surprise and annoyance, found nothing.

The cabo accompanied Alvarez down to the front door and was about to follow him when Alvarez said, 'You'd better stay.'

'Do what?'

'Keep an eye on things.'

'Not likely.'

'Perhaps it would be better if everything is official. I'll have a word with your sargento and make an official request for you to remain, since someone has to.'

'What's stopping you doing the staying?'

'I have to make a personal report to the superior chief.'

Much later, Alvarez silently added as he crossed the drive to his car.

Five

Alvarez came downstairs, walked through the sitting room into the kitchen. Dolores was mixing flour and fat with her hands.

'Have you arrived expecting breakfast or lunch?' she asked. 'You are too late for one, too early for the other.'

'I didn't get back until just before daybreak and I was dead tired so I had a good sleep.'

'And a noisy one. You have been snoring so loudly, it was very disagreeable.'

'I can't help snoring.'

'Of course not, when you drink heavily.'

'Drink has nothing to do with it.'

'As you would deny that drink has anything to do with drunkenness.'

'Women who seldom touch alcohol, snore.'

She attacked the mixture in the bowl. 'It amuses you to insult me?'

'When I said that, I wasn't thinking of you, but—' He stopped abruptly.

'Memories which no decent woman would want to share.'

'I read about it in a magazine.'

'A magazine for those who are interested in how women without shame behave.'

When in her present mood, there was nothing to be gained by further argument. 'I wonder if I could have some breakfast?'

'Something prevents you from getting it?'

It was Jaime's fault that she had failed to understand the woman of the house had a duty to feed the men. 'Are there some ensaimadas or croissants?'

'You suppose I went out at dawn to buy them so that you could eat when you finished snoring? When I had to make certain my children ate well before leaving home?'

He said cravenly, 'Then I'll get something for myself.'

'If you create a mess, you will clear it up.'

He cut two slices of bread, rubbed them with air-dried tomatoes, poured on olive oil. He made coffee. The *pa amb oli* lacked the finesse of taste there would have been had she made it; the coffee tasted unusual. It was not a notable breakfast.

He drove to the post.

'Just climbed out of your coffin?' the duty cabo asked.

Unable to think of a crushing rejoinder, Alvarez showed his contempt for such childish behaviour by silence. He climbed the stairs, paused a moment to regain his breath, went into his office, opened the shutters, sat behind the desk. He was going to have to report to Salas. When young, the superior chief must have been harassed by disconcerted *dimonis boiets*, little demons soured by continuing disbelief in their existence.

He opened the bottom right-hand drawer of his desk, brought out a glass and a bottle of Soberano. On such a day, it seemed only fitting that the bottle was almost empty. He poured half the remaining brandy into the glass and drank. Finally, when there was no valid reason for further hesitation, he dialled Palma.

'Yes?' said the plum-voiced secretary.

'Inspector Alvarez.'

'From where?'

'You know that . . .'

'Were are you phoning from?'

'Llueso.'

'You clearly have not read the superior chief's orders.'

'Of course I have,' he answered, as he looked at the unopened letters on the desk and tried to identify which might be the pertinent one.

'You failed to comprehend that when an inspector rings here, he is to identify himself and then his area? Wait.'

She was said to be unmarried, which should surprise no one. He drank, put the glass down on the desk, studied the bottle. It would provide only one more drink and that as parsimonious as the first. Did he have it now in order to face the immediate future in greater heart, or after the call was over to gain what comfort he could?

'Yes?' said Salas, curtly.

'Inspector Alvarez, señor, speaking from Llueso . . .'

'You imagine I am unaware of that?'

'But I have just been told . . .' He was in danger of admitting he had not read the letter. 'On reading your orders, you wrote—'

'On speaking to my secretary, an inspector was to give his name and area so that she could inform me of both facts when the call was put through. To repeat that information is a waste of my time, which is of great account, and of yours, which is of little.'

Alvarez emptied the bottle into the glass. He drank. Hardly enough to moisten the tongue.

'Well?'

The sudden question startled him and he dropped the receiver on to his lap. On picking it up, he entangled the cord with his wrist. Finally, all was in order.

'You had something more important to do than talk to me?'

'I was startled when you spoke rather sharply and I involuntarily jerked my arm. I suppose I wasn't holding on to the receiver as firmly as I should . . .'

'There is little that you manage to do successfully. Will you now answer my question?'

'I am not quite certain what the question is . . .'

'Are you certain of anything, including the ability your job calls for? Did you not hear me say "Well?" before you threw the phone to the floor?'

'Yes, but I didn't think—'

'Even to a person of limited intelligence, it poses the question, "What is your reason for phoning me?" Answer it and stop wasting even more of my time.'

'During last night, a cabo reported that Señor Heron, an Englishman, had returned home to find his wife was dead in suspicious circumstances.'

'It would not trouble you too much to name where they live?'

'Ca'n Ajo.'

'An absurd name.'

'Not really. The house was built on land which once grew the finest, sweetest garlic. People used to say that one tooth could turn a four-year-old cockerel into a six-month-old pullet and if—'

'Cease wasting time.'

'But you asked me about the name.'

'I remarked that it was an absurd one. I am uninterested in absurdities. Make your report properly.'

'Yes, señor. As I said—'

'Then there is no reason to say it again.'

'Doctor Escarrer from Llueso Health Centre had left Ca'n Ajo before I arrived—'

'Why?'

'He was the doctor on duty and had to hurry back.'

'I was asking why you were not there before he arrived?'

'There must have been some delay in my receiving the information.'

'More likely, in your taking the action the information demanded.'

'He spoke to the cabo before he left. Señora Heron was dead and—'

'To whom are you referring?'

'The wife of the owner of Ca'n Ajo.'

'I am supposed to guess that?'

'I did begin by saying—'

'Absurdities.'

'Doctor Escarrer was of the opinion that the señora had committed suicide.'

'Make out a report in writing and send it to me.'

'I think you should know there is a problem.'

'I expect many when you are in charge of an investigation.'

'There was no gun by her side.'

'It is beyond you to reason that as she fell, a convulsive jerk of the arm cast the gun away under some object?'

'I have carried out a visual search. I can guarantee there is no gun.'

'I would place more faith in a guarantee for a washing machine. You will return and this time make a thorough search.'

'But—'

'Are you incapable of carrying out an order without argument?'

'There was no sign of a suicide note, either.'

'A lack often due to an incompetent search by an incompetent detective who regards it as litter and throws it away.'

'Doctor Noguero arrived soon after we completed our search.'

'Was he surprised to find you there?'

'He is one of the doctors who is licensed to carry out medical forensic work—'

'Might I not be expected to know that?'

'But I understood you wanted everyone to be carefully identified . . . He made a very thorough examination of the dead woman and confirmed she had been shot in one of the elective sites for suicide; there are traces to prove the gun was against her skin when it was fired. She was shot on the right-hand side of her temple, which raises the assumption she was right-handed.'

'Crass incompetence to assume something of such vital importance.'

'There are staff who would have told us, but they weren't around to confirm what her husband said. Since most people are right-handed, it seems likely she was.'

'You are told not to work on assumption, yet proceed immediately to continue to do so.'

'When the fact is—'

'A fact is only a fact when it is proved to be. Unless confirmed, you will not repeat this assumption when I receive your report by the end of the morning.'

'This morning?'

'You imagine I am referring to one day next week?'

'But I've hardly had any sleep.'

'That is no excuse for laziness. There is reason for once

to hope your report will be comprehensible since the case
is clearly straightforward.' He cut the connection.

Alvarez hesitated, replaced the receiver to re-engage a
line, dialled.

'Yes?'

'Inspector Alvarez from Llueso. I would like to speak to
the superior chief again.'

There was a brief pause before Salas said, 'What the
devil is it now?'

'The death of Señora Heron was not suicide, señor.'

'It is medically determined she shot herself, yet you wish
to claim it was not suicide. There have been times when I
have wondered how your mind works. I now doubt that it
does.'

'I was about to give further evidence when you cut me off.'

'I had no interest in your sleeping habits.'

'Doctor Noguero made a much more thorough examination of the dead woman than Doctor Escarrer. That is
logical since—'

'Leave logical explanations to those capable of delivering
them.'

'He found there was a second bullet wound in her thigh,
which in his opinion had been fired from a distance. At
this stage it is impossible to be certain, but as Doctor
Noguero said, the most likely course of events was that
the first shot, fired from a distance, was aimed at her
heart, but since accuracy with a pistol, which one pre-
sumes was the weapon used, is very difficult, hit her in
the thigh. This caused her to collapse to the ground and
then she was approached and the gun put to her head and
fired.'

'In the most convoluted manner, you are saying that she
was murdered?'

'Since she could not have shot herself from a distance—'

'You do accept that?'

'I am about to return to Ca'n Ajo to speak to the staff,
if they are there now.'

'That would be difficult if they are not. Why have you
not already questioned them?'

'As I mentioned, I didn't return home until well after four this morning—'

'It is astonishing how many excuses you find for sheer inefficiency. Since Heron reported the murder of his wife, experience suggests he will become the prime suspect. Have you confirmed that he is?'

'Not so far.'

'You are intending to question him again before the end of the month?'

'Naturally, señor.'

'Little is natural when you are concerned. You will question Heron very firmly and confirm or deny what he tells you. How many staff are there?'

'I don't know yet.'

'Remiss of me to think you might. You will conduct a thorough search of the house to find the murder weapon. If that fails, you will scour every centimetre of the grounds since it is common practice for a criminal to get rid of incriminating evidence with panicky haste.'

'The garden is rather large.'

'Why is that of any consequence?'

'To search it closely will take a long time and you have asked me to do so much else. A day has only twenty-four hours.'

'The quality of your work leads me to believe that a day has far fewer.'

Six

In daylight, the garden at Ca'n Ajo was far more attractive than the house, as Alvarez had suspected the night before. There again were the lawns providing a sharp contrast to the brown countryside beyond; late-flowering Judas trees; hedges of lantana and red and white oleanders; yellow, white and red hibiscus; flowerbeds filled with colour; plumbago showing early speckles of blue; pergolas entwined with climbing roses; the curved rock fountain had a metre-tall spray which was sparkled by the sun; and as a perfect backdrop, mountains with their own austere beauty. Close to the surrounding pines, a man was working at the one empty oblong bed with a mattock, the tool universally used for hand cultivation of land, despite the advantages of a fork or spade.

Alvarez crossed from his car to where the other stood. 'You work here, then?'

'Me? Just sit all day, reading the paper.'

'I'm Inspector Alvarez of the Cuerpo.'

'And there was me thinking you'd come to try and sell me something I already had.'

Years ago, no one would have dared to show such open contempt for authority. Yet contempt would have been there. A spirit of independence was one of the greatest gifts men could have. 'What's your name?'

'Diego Ferrer.'

'You're here full-time?'

'You reckon an hour a day would keep things looking as they are?'

'Who else works here?'

'No one.'

'No staff in the house?'

'Thought you were talking about the garden.'

He had, of course, thought no such thing. 'So who's in the house?'

'You asking who works there, or who lives there?'

Alvarez smiled. 'Let's agree you're not as stupid as you're trying to make out and answer the question.'

Ferrer was annoyed that he was meeting good humour, not sharp annoyance. 'The wife and Teresa.'

'No other staff in a house of that size?'

'She wouldn't pay for anyone more, like she wouldn't give me any help. Didn't care if it killed me trying to keep up with the work.'

'You look a long way from dying.'

'Can't say the same for you.'

A spiteful comment, not a reasoned judgement. Yet there had been times recently when Alvarez had wondered if he were more breathless than usual after some physical action. 'When you said "she", presumably you meant Señora Heron?'

'Wanted two euros' work for one euro's pay.'

'A typical employer.'

'She weren't typical of anything. A real bitch.'

Alvarez was surprised. It was customary for death to wash away a person's failings, at least for a few weeks. 'She complained a lot?'

Ferrer rested the blade of the mattock on the ground and leaned awkwardly on the end of the curved handle. 'Them that pays, complains. But she behaved like she lived in a *possessió* and we was in drystone huts along with the animals.'

'And is the señor the same?'

'Couldn't be more different. She could speak some Spanish, but wouldn't; he can't, but tries and laughs when he gets it all wrong. Meet him in the village and he'll try to have a chat; meet her and she won't see you. Only listened to herself. Told me to plant things in July and August, even when I said that was stupid. They died off, no matter how much I watered them, and so according to her, I was no good at me job. No good when I've been at it for years!'

'At least she couldn't complain about the garlic. Even a foreigner couldn't find fault in that.'

'So why did she tell me to clear all of it, growing and stored, and throw it away?'

Alvarez expressed his shocked astonishment at so profane an act in several of the more vivid Mallorquin phrases.

'You know why she wanted rid of it?'

'She was out of her mind?'

'Because she was a witch.'

'You mean bitch?'

'I mean what I says.'

'People used to say garlic became fire in a witch's stomach and consumed her. But that's about as likely as travelling around on broomsticks. Wouldn't be safe these days with all the aeroplanes, anyway.'

'Seems like you've never heard of Catalina Bagur and Matilde Lopez who lived on the side of Puig Antonia.'

'They had a broomstick party?'

'Catalina had been widowed, so she kept chickens and sold the eggs in the market. Best eggs one could buy because all around her house were bits and pieces for the birds to eat. Matilde bought half a dozen one Sunday in the market, after arguing about the price. Next Sunday she was back, saying three of the eggs had been bad and she wanted three fresh ones to make up for them. Catalina had a temper – so her husband said many a time before he died – and was rightly proud of the eggs she sold and she shouted so as people could hear that Matilde was lying to get something for nothing. People laughed and jeered at Matilde – no one liked her – and she swore Catalina would regret her words. That night, all the chickens died. You know why?'

'Coccidiosis?'

Ferrer hawked and spat to show his contempt for such stupidity. 'With them dead, Catalina didn't have anything to make the few pesetas she needed to stay alive. So she decided to kill herself and be with her husband once more. But first, she'd get her own back on the witch. She put some garlic in Matilde's food before she hanged herself with an old belt of her husband's.

'A lad from Llueso wanted a love potion – lads from your village have never been strong – so he went along to Matilde's house. Couldn't raise her so had a look around and found her dead in the earth closet. And you want to say there aren't witches?'

'Unless you can tell me how Catalina managed to slip garlic into the food which Matilde ate when witchcraft should have told her it was there, then yes, I say there aren't witches.'

'You blokes wouldn't believe an angel.'

Alvarez indicated the ground Ferrer was cultivating. 'What are you going to plant there?'

'More miniature roses, she said. Wrong time of year, I said. If she told me what to plant, I was to plant it. Didn't matter they'd be sickly and die.'

'Now she's dead, you can plant garlic.'

'There ain't any to plant.'

'There what?'

'I told you, I had to throw all of it away.'

'You want me to believe you didn't keep some back?'

'She'd eyes so sharp, being a witch, she'd spot a pebble on top of a mountain.'

'And you weren't smart enough to squirrel away a bagful of cloves where she couldn't see 'em, even if her eyes were like Zeiss binoculars?'

Ferrer raised the mattock, brought it down so that the blade dug into the soil, pulled it backwards to break up the earth. 'Wanting some garlic, aren't you?'

'Have I asked you for any?'

'All your talk is coming round to asking.'

'You're completely mistaken,' Alvarez said with pompous dignity. 'And I'll tell you why. The land belongs to the señor and he pays you for your time, so what you grow is his. You don't have the right to give any away and as a member of the Cuerpo I am not going to encourage such a breach of the law.'

'So if I was to offer you half a dozen cloves, you'd refuse 'em?'

'You threw it all away so there's nothing to offer.'

'Spinach leaves give good cover.'

Despite the earlier denials, it seemed likely Ferrer had continued to grow garlic, so the inferred offer might be genuine. Yet Ferrer was cunning and might have been making a spurious offer in the hope Alvarez would accept it and by doing so, admit that his regard for the law had limitations.

'If you don't want 'em . . .'

That Ferrer was now pressing the offer made Alvarez certain his suspicions were correct. 'Right now I have more important things to worry about.'

'You don't seem in a hurry.'

'I have to find out what happened.'

'She blows her head off, that's what.'

'That's not what. She was murdered.'

Ferrer released his hold on the mattock, stood upright, scratched the back of his neck with earthy fingers. 'Not surprising.'

'A strange thing to say.'

'Everyone disliked her.'

'Including you?'

'You try spending all day working as hard as you can – which probably ain't so hard – and then have her come along and complain you've been wasting your time and her money.'

'Does "everyone" include the señor?'

'Probably, since he'd every cause.'

'That's a rough thing to say.'

'I speak as I find. She was always complaining about him as well as us. Like the time his friends came to a party.' He paused, continued reflectively: 'Most of 'em were nice people, even if they was foreigners.'

'They told you how wonderful the garden looked?'

'Don't stop 'em being nice.' Ferrer searched the pockets of the ancient trousers he wore. 'Me fags must have dropped out.'

Like hell they had! 'Have one of mine.' He produced a pack of Fortunas and offered it.

'Usually smoke Pall Mall,' Ferrer observed as he took a cigarette.

'How the rich live!' Alvarez drew out a cigarette for himself, pocketed the pack, lit a match for them both. 'You were going to tell me how she complained about the señor when his friends came to a party.'

'No, I wasn't. And it was after.'

'What happened?'

'I was dead-heading some roses and heard 'em because the windows were wide open. They was having a row. Leastwise, she was. Said his friends had been rude and acting like they were so superior. The señor tried to tell her she was wrong. They was talking about hunting and fishing because they lived in the country and that's what they liked doing. Said she didn't understand country people and that made her real mad. She'd paid for all they'd eaten and drunk and she wasn't going to waste another euro on them or him.'

'There's something I don't understand. You obviously understand English, yet made out you didn't.'

'Didn't make out anything.'

'If the señor had to speak to you in broken Spanish, obviously he thought you didn't understand English. Why didn't you tell him you did?'

'He never asked.'

'More likely you were acting dumb so that when they talked carelessly, you'd learn something which could be useful to you.'

'I ain't wasting any more time talking to someone with a mind as twisted as yours.'

'And I have to go into the house and have a chat with the señor, Teresa and your wife.'

'You think you're going to upset her with your talk?' Ferrer demanded aggressively.

'I'm hoping all three will be able to help me, as you have.'

'You leave me out of it.'

Alvarez turned, walked past the northern end of the nearer pergola, crossed the lawn and drive, stepped into the over-stated porch, rang the bell.

The door was opened by a woman who still enjoyed late youth because she had not had to work in the fields for many hours in the sunshine alongside her parents. She had blonde hair – dark at the roots – high forehead, light blue eyes, awkward nose, thin mouth, square chin. Very unlikely to be Ferrer's wife. 'Are you Teresa?'

'Yes.'

Her expression became wary.

He introduced himself in friendly terms. She seemed bewildered by events. Unlike the many old people who had known the war, violent death for her was uncommon and therefore frightening. 'May I come in?' He stepped into the hall, closed the door. 'Is the señor home?'

'Yes.'

'I'd like to have a word with him.'

She said nothing.

'Where is he?'

'In the sitting room.'

'Then I'll go there. I know the way.'

He crossed the hall and entered the large room. Sunlight was sweeping through the opened windows, guarded by mosquito netting, and brought life even to the granite-framed fireplace.

As before, Heron sat facing the dead television set. He had not shaved, brushed his hair or changed his clothes. On the small table by his side was a half-filled glass, a bottle of whisky and an ice bucket; on the floor was a disordered broadsheet newspaper and opened book.

'What is it?' he demanded heavily.

'Good morning, señor.'

He turned to face Alvarez. 'Thought . . . thought it was Teresa.' He stood slowly. 'Sorry; very rude.'

It was distressing yet perversely risible to see a man suffering from emotional trauma who was trying to maintain social courtesy.

'I must again apologize for troubling you, but I have to ask some more questions.'

Heron looked away. 'You'll have a drink?'

Alvarez hesitated, but it occurred to him that Heron

wished to replenish his own glass, but did not like to do so unaccompanied. 'Thank you, I should like a small one.'

'Whisky?'

'Please. With just ice.'

Heron stood, almost lost his balance, steadied himself by holding on to a chair, poured out a whisky, added two cubes of ice, sat, drank.

Shock could have strange affects on a person, Alvarez thought sadly. Heron was trying to be a good host, yet was drinking the whisky Alvarez had been offered . . .

'I must apologize,' Heron said abruptly.

Alvarez's hopes rose.

'Last night I . . . I created a bit of a scene.'

'I would never describe what happened as such.'

'I saw the terrible wound, yet couldn't believe she was dead, but when I went and touched her . . .' He drank, stared into the past.

'Señor, can you tell me now what happened yesterday evening, or would you prefer to wait a short time?'

'I've said.'

'I fear we must go over it again. You returned home after midnight?'

'I . . . I can't give a time.'

'You phoned the police at quarter to one. You had been out on your own?'

'Yes.'

'Then your wife had remained in the house?'

'She wasn't here.'

'I don't understand.'

He drank heavily. 'Not talking straight. Not thinking straight. She wasn't meant to return that early, so when I found the front door unlocked I thought . . .'

'You thought you had been burgled a second time?'

'Yes.'

'Where had your wife been?'

'England.'

'When did you expect her to return?'

'I was to collect her from the airport. She had an early morning flight.'

'Today – Friday?'

'I suppose so.'

'You found the door unlocked. Did that not suggest to you that she might have returned sooner than expected?'

'Just thought we'd been burgled again.'

'You have mentioned that. When did that happen?'

'A couple of months ago, I think.'

'You lost some pieces of silver and most of your electronic gear. So this time you searched the house to see if anything else was missing. I looked for the key to your wife's safe, but failed to find it. Now I would like your permission to have a locksmith open the safe.'

Heron nodded.

'Not expecting your wife to return until the next day, you had spent part or all of the evening down in the port at one of the front cafés. Which one was that?'

Heron finished his drink, poured himself another, drank. His hand was shaking.

'If you would tell me, then I can leave you in peace.' Alvarez cursed himself for using an expression so clumsy in the circumstances.

'What's it matter?'

'At the moment I can't say, but it might become important.'

'How in hell do you expect me to remember?'

'I am hoping you will. Do you have a favourite front café?'

After a long pause, he said, 'I suppose so.'

'The name?'

'Pascual.'

'So it's quite probable you went there?'

'I suppose so.'

Alvarez stood. 'I am most grateful, señor, for your kindness in helping me in this most sad of times for you.'

He left the room, checked the time. Well after midday. He had intended to talk to Ferrer's wife and Teresa, but to do so now must interfere with their lunch; he would return home for his.

*   *   *

'You're back early,' was Dolores's greeting.

'I didn't want to be late again,' he answered, hoping his thoughtfulness would win favour with her.

'No bored young foreign women around, I suppose.' She returned to the kitchen.

He sat at the table, brought out a bottle of brandy and glass, poured himself a drink. He would have liked ice, but that demanded he went into the kitchen and faced Dolores in her present challenging mood.

Heron had been distraught the previous night, barely composed this morning. That was to be expected and yet . . .

Dolores walked through the bead curtain. 'You have nothing better to do than drink?'

'I was thinking.'

'But not that you could help me by laying the table.'

Would women soon expect men to do all the housework? He sighed, put down his glass and stood to do as he was bid.

Seven

Alvarez arrived back at Ca'n Ajo later than intended, but he had really needed the long siesta. Teresa opened the front door and told him the señor was probably still in the sitting room, but she couldn't be certain. He was in a terrible state. Eva had cooked a meal for him, but he had eaten practically nothing, even though it had been one of his favourite dishes.

Realizing Eva must be Ferrer's wife, he asked, 'What was the meal?' as he stepped into the hall.

'*Patata rellenas*.'

'Eva is a good cook?'

'Brilliant.'

Then the scooped-out potatoes, filled with a mixture of ham, onion, parsley, mushrooms, eggs, butter, shallots and stock, might almost have rivalled anything Dolores could magic up ... If he had been married and found his wife murdered, he hoped the bitter grief wouldn't deaden his appetite.

'You said you want to speak to the señor again?'

'I didn't. This time it's you and the others.'

'Why me?' She spoke in a rush of words. 'I don't know anything. Honest to God, I don't.'

'Of course you don't, not directly, that is. But you may be able to tell me something which doesn't seem of any importance to you, but might be to me.'

He was assuming her innocence because she was female, young, Mallorquin, and it was difficult to imagine her deliberately hurting anyone. Yet, life was changing and womanhood no longer meant sweet innocence; women had invaded men's territory.

'What do you want to know, then?' she asked, more calmly.

'Maybe we could go somewhere where we can sit and have a chat?'

'The others are in the kitchen having coffee.'

'Then why not join them?'

She hesitated, then led the way across the hall, down a passage, and into a large kitchen that appeared to Alvarez to have been equipped with every device on the market.

Ferrer and Eva were seated at the table on which were mugs, a coffee machine, milk, sugar, plates, and half a chocolate sponge.

He judged Eva to be roughly the same age as her husband, which was to be expected of someone of her generation; her black hair was drawn tightly back into a bun, her face was round, her dark eyes possessed a beauty that was missing in the rest of her features. She stared up at Alvarez, defensively curious.

'Inspector Alvarez, Cuerpo,' he said.

'And isn't that a coincidence?' Ferrer spoke sarcastically as he held a large piece of sponge in front of his mouth.

'Why'd you say that?' Eva asked.

'His turning up when there's food on the table.'

'Don't talk stupid.' She turned to Alvarez. 'If it's the señor you want . . .'

'Not this time.'

'I've told you why he's here,' Ferrer said, through a mouthful of sponge.

'Your tongue's too busy,' she snapped.

'I have to ask you a few questions to find out what life is like here,' Alvarez said.

'Like anywhere else.'

Despite the surrounding wealth? The murder? Yet since the wealth was not theirs and she appeared far less distressed than Teresa, perhaps life as she saw it was not very unusual.

'Why don't you sit down and have some of my sponge cake?' There was a touch of pride in her voice.

He sat.

'I can make you some fresh coffee, if you'd like?'

'If that's not too much trouble . . .'

'No trouble where he's concerned,' Ferrer said sourly as he watched Alvarez pull closer to himself the plate on which sat the sponge.

Alvarez had had a piece of cake and two cups of coffee before leaving home, but to refuse her generous offer would have appeared ungrateful, even rude. He cut a large slice.

The sponge was as light as an angel's wing beat; the chocolate filling and coating, rich perfection.

Eva poured him a mug of coffee and put it in front of him. 'How do you find my sponge?' she asked.

Women would not accept the slightest reservation. 'I have never eaten better.'

She beamed her approval. 'Then have some more.'

He did so.

'I thought you were here to ask questions, not eat and drink,' Ferrer said, annoyed by the amount Alvarez was eating.

'Didn't I ask him if he'd like some coffee and a little of my sponge?' Eva snapped.

'Can't have heard you say "little".'

Alvarez swallowed a last mouthful of sponge. 'Can you say if the señora was right-handed?'

'I'm pretty certain she was,' Teresa said immediately.

'I can be certain she was.' Eva made it clear Teresa was too unreliable for her answer to be accepted unreservedly.

'That's one problem out of the way. Maybe now you'd like to tell me about the señor and señora?'

They looked at each other. Teresa said, 'How d'you mean?'

'For a start, was it reasonably pleasant working here?'

'Like I've said, he was all right,' Teresa said hesitantly. 'Just it was difficult to understand him some times. But she was a—'

'There's no call to speak bad about her now she's dead,' Eva said sharply.

'Being dead don't alter anything.'

Ferrer hastened to support his wife. 'You ought to have more respect than to speak like that.'

'You were critical of her this morning,' Alvarez reminded him.

'Never said much.' He reached across the table to seize the small remaining piece of sponge before Alvarez had it.

'You suggested she had a sharp tongue.'

'She could go on.'

'With cause,' Eva said sharply, 'since you never learned how to be subtle. You wanted something done your way, you told her that's how it should be, instead of agreeing with what she said and then doing what you wanted.'

'She was obviously a very difficult person,' Alvarez remarked. 'Nothing was ever right.'

'There were times when she could be—' She stopped abruptly.

'A real bitch,' Teresa finished for her.

'How can you talk like that?'

'I've heard you call her that many a time.'

'When she was alive.'

'Being dead doesn't change what kind of person she was.'

'Have you no respect?'

Alvarez hastened to defuse a possible row. 'Relations between her and the señor must have become strained at times?'

Teresa began to answer. 'You should have heard her when—'

'It's not something to talk about,' Eva said sharply. 'You're here to work, not repeat bits of gossip.'

'He asked me, didn't he? He's a detective, isn't he?'

'I'm afraid I have to know,' Alvarez said, 'even though I dislike discussing other people's lives as much as you so rightly do.'

Eva was mollified, but determined to try to prevent Teresa's answering the question. 'The señor is the kind of man a woman would think herself lucky enough to marry. But she . . . you say you have to know, so I'll tell you. When she spoke to him, it was as if she was speaking to one of us, working for the money she paid; he spoke to her as if all was right between them whatever she said. He has more patience than me.'

'What she needed was his right hand to calm her down,' Ferrer said.

'You think a husband has the right to hit his wife?' Eva demanded aggressively.

'In the old days . . .'

'These aren't the old days.'

Dolores and Eva could not have been more different in appearance, Alvarez thought, but there was a similarity in character. An assumption of equality with – even superiority over – men. How could that have been allowed to happen?

'So you'd call him a kind, caring husband?'

'Very much so.'

'It was his nature to be friendly and kind?'

'I've just said, haven't I?'

'I wondered if, since I understand she had more money than he does, he decided he had to treat her pleasantly, however she treated him.'

'He'd have been the same if he'd had all the money,' Teresa said.

The phone by the side of the breadmaker rang. Ferrer stood, crossed to it, lifted the receiver. In between periods of listening, he said in perfectly comprehensible English that Señor Heron was too distressed to speak to anyone. He would pass on to Señor Heron the señora's kind condolences. He replaced the receiver. 'That was Señora Adler.' He wrote the name down on a sheet of paper.

'Is she the woman with long red hair who always has a friendly chat if she sees us?' Teresa asked.

'That's Señora Knox,' Ferrer answered as he sat. 'Señora Adler is one long streak of misery. Always suffering from something and insists on telling you all about it.'

'The señora had many friends?' Alvarez asked.

'She was always giving parties; never thought about all the extra work that meant for us. And never a word of thanks, even when Eva and me had been cleaning up at two in the morning,' said Ferrer.

'Me as well,' Teresa said.

'I have the impression,' Alvarez said, 'that they had different kinds of friends.'

'Like *vino de casa* and Marqués de Riscal,' Ferrer replied.

A comparison Alvarez appreciated since Riscal was one of his favourite, more expensive wines. 'His friends were more like the English used to be when there weren't hoards of tourists?'

'Wouldn't know about that, but they were friendly.'

'And her friends?'

'The last party she gave,' Teresa said, 'I was serving and one of 'em pinched my bum.'

'No doubt you gave cause,' Eva said.

'Even you might get your bum pinched if you were handing round drinks and eats,' said Ferrer.

'As if they'd dare!' Teresa had made her disbelief that anyone would bother Eva rather too obvious, and now shrank under Eva's icy glare.

'Have you ever noticed any ill feeling between guests and the señora?'

They looked at each other. 'Can't say so,' Ferrer answered.

'And as far as you know, the señora was never threatened by anyone?'

'Nothing like that, was there?' He looked at his wife. She shook her head.

'She didn't receive any phone calls which upset her?'

'Can't remember any,' Eva replied.

'It was making 'em that used to make her really bitchy,' Teresa said.

'I've told you not to speak about her like that.'

Teresa was unabashed. 'I can remember you saying just that after she made one call and then told you the meat at lunch had been tough and tasteless.'

Alvarez hastened to calm matters. 'Have you any idea whether the calls that troubled her were always to the same person?'

Teresa shook her head.

'Did you ever gain any idea of what the problem was?'

'You think I listened to what she said on the phone?'

'Not deliberately, but sometimes one chances—'

'It was always in English so I couldn't have understood even if I had heard anything. All I know is that after the last one she made, she was like she'd gone crazy. Maybe she had, because it was after that she gave us all time off.'

'Which was unusual?'

'Never happened before.'

'Why do you think she did so?'

'How would I know?'

'That she did once surely means she wasn't a complete virago?'

'If you'd worked for her, you'd know the answer to that.'

'Have any of you noticed any strangers hanging around the place recently?'

'The road's used, but there's been no one in the grounds, not that I've seen,' Ferrer said.

Alvarez picked up his mug, found it was empty.

'You'd like some more coffee?' Eva asked.

'That's very kind.' He handed her the mug.

'You think maybe in a while I could have a little more?' Ferrer asked sarcastically.

'Shouldn't you be getting back to work?'

'You think he'll be worrying about what I'm doing when he's sitting in front of the television what's not switched on?'

'That should not stop you working when you're meant to.'

A very difficult woman. Alvarez said, 'One last thing. I need a photograph of the señor.'

Teresa was the first to ask, 'What for?'

'To help my investigation.'

'How's it going to do that?'

'One can never be certain.'

'Where are we supposed to get a photograph of him?'

'Isn't there one in the bedroom, the sitting room, the library?'

'There's him on a horse.'

'That will do.'

'I can't take it without asking him.'

'You have my authority to get it.'

She hesitated.

'I'll return it before he even knows it's been missing.'

'If the inspector says it's all right, it maybe is,' Ferrer said.

Teresa left the room, returning several minutes later with a coloured photograph which she handed to Alvarez. In the foreground a younger, smiling Heron was leaning over the neck of the horse on which he was seated to accept a small glass from an elegantly dressed woman. In the background were many horses and people. Fox-hunting. Said to be very dangerous.

Alvarez used his mobile to phone the Policia Local in Port Llueso. 'I'm hoping you can give me some information.'

'Now there's an optimist!'

'Two and a half months ago, Señor Heron, who lives at Ca'n Ajo—'

'Is that the place built on the garlic field?'

'It is.'

The policia detailed what he would do to the man who had sold the field, the man who had bought it and built on it, the bureaucrats who had given permission to build. Alvarez agreed that no punishment could be sufficiently awesome to make them suffer enough. They discussed the magic in each garlic tooth; they reminisced about the notable meals it had enabled them to enjoy.

Twenty minutes later, the policia said, 'Weren't you asking about something?'

'The robbery at Ca'n Ajo.'

'That's it. Hang on and I'll see if someone bothered to make a report.'

He returned to the phone. 'May the thirty-first of this year. Señor Heron reported a break-in and Damián Crespi went along. The usual local heist – television, computer, video, DVD, a couple of silver teapots and some other small pieces of silver.

'I remember Damián said how it was odd – a safe in each of two bedrooms and she wouldn't let the husband open one of them, but had to do it herself. Makes one wonder what she kept in there . . .'

'Did you clear up the case?'

'Reckoned it had to be Cortes, but couldn't wrap him up in it. He's small time, but smart enough not to have left anything around except the usual marks.'

'What marks?'

'He's designed some sort of tool which opens shutters with no problem; leaves a pattern of indentations in the wood.'

'You questioned him?'

'Until we were exhausted. Searched his house, asked around who was selling cheap electronic gear and small silver articles, got nowhere.'

Alvarez thanked the other and rang off, ready for whatever delicacy Dolores had prepared after a long day's work.

Eight

Café Pascual was separated from the beach only by a pedestrianized road. Alvarez made his way between the outside tables, at which sat holidaymakers, many in swimming costumes, sheltered by sun umbrellas, and into the interior. Few were sitting inside.

Valls, squat, bald, harassed, was arguing with the bartender. He turned and stared angrily at Alvarez, who began to introduce himself. 'You think I don't know who you are? What do you want here?'

'Your help.'

'And if you knew how to balance four trays on your arms and one on your head, I'd need yours. Still not eleven, outside tables filled with people demanding service all at the same time, and I have a bartender who wants to quit because he says he has a pain in the stomach.'

'It's like a shark is gnawing at it,' said the bartender.

'More like a rat.'

A waiter hurried up to the bar. 'Two coñacs, three beers, one gin and tonic.' He put down a tray.

'I've got to see a doctor,' said the bartender.

'You've got to pour drinks.'

'I have the right to cease work in order to consult a doctor.' The bartender left.

Valls hurried around the bar, gathered up six glasses. 'His right!' He picked up a bottle of gin. 'What about my right to have him do the job he's paid for?' He poured out two measures.

'Emilio,' the waiter observed, 'pours a fuller measure than you.'

'Which is why I'm running this place at a loss.'

'And it's one gin, two coñacs.'

Valls swore, picked up a fresh glass, poured out the brandies, added ice. He brought one bottle of tonic and three of beer from the refrigerator, put them on a tray.

As the waiter left, another arrived and asked for two brandies and two *cafés con leche*. There was further swearing when Valls had trouble persuading the espresso machine to work. He used a handkerchief to mop the sweat from his face.

'You need to get into better shape,' Alvarez observed.

'And you need to eff off.'

'I will as soon as I've had a word with the staff.'

'You still don't understand you're in the sodding way?'

'Then I'll move outside and amuse myself by counting the tables.'

'What are you on about now?'

'They're set so close together I'm wondering if you've put out more than your permit allows?'

'You're Cuerpo, so what's that to do with you?'

'Nothing. But the policia may be interested . . .'

'You're a bastard.'

'Who has a job to do.'

'And—'

A waiter interrupted him. 'Four beers.'

Valls put four chilled bottles of beer on the tray. 'There's only three left so get along to the back and bring a couple of cases.'

'There's too many customers shouting.' The waiter picked up the tray and hurried away.

'I'll have a heart attack before the day's out.' Valls turned to leave and collect the beer.

'It'll only take a moment with each man.'

'What's it you want of them?'

'To show each one a photograph of a man and ask if he saw him here on Thursday evening.'

'With this place in a riot every evening, you expect them to remember someone from when there was a festival on?'

'Hopefully.'

'Then you're blind crazy.'

And wasting my time, Alvarez thought later when none of the waiters could remember who had been at the café on Thursday night.

Seated behind his desk at the post, Alvarez considered life. On the plus side, it was Saturday and it was his habit to start his weekend at lunchtime. On the minus side, he had an ongoing case on which he might be expected to work throughout the two days.

He recalled Pedro Esteban's wise words: 'Alcohol is a panacea. It brings heart to the timid, hope to the worried, optimism to the pessimist.' He brought a new bottle of brandy and a glass out of the bottom drawer and poured himself a drink. He phoned Palma.

'Yes?' said a female voice which was not that of the plum-voiced secretary.

'I'd like to speak to Señor—' The line briefly went dead.

'Yes?'

'Is that Señor Salas?'

'You ring my office and expect to speak to the inspector general?'

'No, but I wanted to make certain you were you.'

'You frequently speak to someone who is not the person to whom you are speaking?'

'Señor, your usual secretary did not answer my call and so she didn't know who I was . . .'

'You consider that strange?'

'What I meant was, if she wasn't here, I mean there, your office—'

'Is there the slightest chance you could speak intelligibly?'

'I was referring to whoever it was that did answer. I didn't have time to give my name and she didn't ask who I was before she put the call through so I wasn't certain to whom I was speaking . . .'

'Conversing with you can be likened to attempting to understand Euscaro. You will now speak as coherently as possible, accept I am who I am, and explain why you have phoned.'

'I have carried out extensive inquiries, speaking to many people—'

'You see no need initially to identify the purpose of your inquiries so I have some small chance of understanding you?'

'The murder of Señora Heron.'

'Then we now have a starting point to your report.'

There was a silence.

'We have the ending as well?' Salas asked.

'I thought you were going to say something more, señor.'

'There is much I would like to say were it not unsuitable for a senior officer to address his junior in such terms. Make your report before it becomes history.'

'I spoke to Señor Heron. His evidence basically remains unchanged. Once again, initially he could not – or would not – say where he had been before he returned to Ca'n Ajo, but I pressed him to tell me. He had not expected his wife back from England until the early hours of the morning, so he went down to the port and had a drink or two at Café Pascual. He returned home before intending to drive to the airport later, found the front door unlocked, which made him fear he had been burgled again, searched downstairs, went upstairs and found his wife dead.

'In order to substantiate his evidence, I drove down to the café to ask the staff if anyone could remember him being there, or equally, could be certain he had not been. Of course, I realized the unlikelihood of meeting any success, given how busy the port was on Thursday evening.'

'You always identify failure before you meet it?'

'As you have often said, señor, a negative can be as positive as a positive. At that time of night and this time of the year, Café Pascual, like all the other front cafés, is filled with so many people, the waiters are so busy, that Señor Heron might have been there and no one noticed him. Especially since it was the Festival of the Fishermen. On the other hand, since he is frequently there, one might expect him, despite the crush of people, to have been recognized if there. Of course, when asked to pin down the sighting to a certain hour on a certain day, it does seem a lot less

likely there could be success. So the negative can hardly
be positive—'

'Translate.'

'I don't understand . . .'

'My problem precisely. To reach some coherency, restrict
yourself to answering one question. Do you believe Heron
was, or was not, at the café at the time of the señora's
death?'

'That has to depend on whether or not he needed to
explain where he had been.'

'Did he?'

'Did he what?'

'I think I must start at the beginning again. Have you
learned anything to help identify the murderer?'

'I fear not.'

'You are aware that one of the main causes of domestic
murder is aggression between the spouses?'

'Yes, señor. In fact, I believe—'

'Do not obscure matters. Have you thought to find out
what was the relationship between Heron and his wife?'

'I have spoken to the staff and they agree that she was
a dislikable woman who was often very unpleasant to her
husband, especially when the subject was money.'

'Why that?'

'She had far more than he.'

'Do the known facts lead you to any provisional conclusion?'

'Not really.'

'If a couple dislike each other, the wife has more money
than he and so with typical female spite makes him
constantly aware of the fact, if it is he who finds her body
and he provides an alibi which – according to you – cannot
be confirmed, you would not agree he should be the prime
suspect?'

'Señor, I agree with what you say, but—'

'But what?'

'I questioned the staff at Ca'n Ajo and without exception they believe the señor incapable of harming his wife
and to have been greatly shocked by her death.'

'Of little account.'

'There's something . . . As you have frequently said, señor, if in a case something is out of rhythm, one needs to consider it carefully.'

'When I have made that point, I have done so far more perspicaciously.'

'Before she died, she gave the staff time off. It was completely unlike her to do something like that, so why did she?'

'Your conclusion?'

'I haven't yet reached one.'

'Then move on to something about which you might have some relevant knowledge. Who are the other suspects?'

'Provisionally, there is only one at the moment.'

'What does "provisionally" indicate?'

'Ca'n Ajo was robbed back in May. I've had a word with the policia local and they suspected the guilty man was Cortes, but failed to find evidence to warrant his arrest. He's a small-timer, lacking the skills needed to force the two safes in Ca'n Ajo. However, it has to be possible he returned with an accomplice who did have those skills and they were interrupted by the señora.'

'You have questioned him?'

'Not yet.'

'Why not?'

'I decided the first thing to do was to find out if any of the señora's jewellery had been stolen.'

'Had it?'

'Since the señor gave me permission to ask a locksmith to force the safe, I did not need your permission—'

'You waste both our times by telling me what I know.'

'The locksmith will be at Ca'n Ajo as soon as possible.'

'Which should have been much sooner.' Salas hung up.

Nine

Dolores stepped through the bead curtain into the sitting room. She looked at Alvarez and Jaime. 'Perhaps I should not have bothered to prepare a meal. Isabel and Juan are eating with friends and so there was only myself to consider. I am content with a little cold meat and salad.'

Jaime looked at Alvarez for support and received none. 'How d'you mean, there wasn't anyone to consider?'

'I said, there was only myself.'

'But we have to eat.'

'You are having a liquid lunch.'

'This is only my second drink.'

'You have an unusual system of counting.'

'Maybe I did have a very small one first.'

She stared at the almost empty bottle. 'Was that not unopened when you sat down?'

'I don't remember,' Jaime answered lamely. 'Anyway, Enrique's been having some as well.'

'One drink,' Alvarez corrected.

'More strange counting! The meal will be ready in five minutes. Do not hesitate to say that you are not hungry and cannot be bothered to eat what has taken me so long to prepare.'

'Forgo the delicious meal you're cooking?' Alvarez said, expressing much amazement.

'Very well. But you will eat when it is ready.' She returned to the kitchen.

They drank.

'Isabel gained *sobresaliente* for arithmetic yesterday,' Jaime said.

'That's good.'

'She's clever.'

'Naturally, being a woman,' Dolores remarked as she stepped back into the room. She spoke to Alvarez. 'Have you yet rung Riba?'

'Why?'

'Your memory has already flown on an alcoholic cloud? I told you he had rung twice and asked you to get in touch with him as soon as possible.'

'I don't remember you telling me that.'

'Had you stopped less often on your return here, perhaps your memory would fare better.'

'I did not go into a single bar.'

'But sat outside several.'

'I came straight back. What's Old Lorenzo want?'

'You imagine the caller was Old Lorenzo? That he would ask to speak to you after you scorned his daughter even though she had asked me what were your favourite foods and would I be so very kind as to show her how to prepare them?'

'Only a blind masochist would marry her.'

'Not an elderly man who is unable to understand that he amuses, not excites, young women?' She returned to the kitchen.

'So who is this Riba who telephoned?' Alvarez called after Dolores's retreating back, but she decided not to hear him.

Jaime spoke in a low voice. 'I suppose you didn't hear her mention Riba because you were thinking of a blonde.'

'I'm certain she never mentioned Riba to me.'

'You wouldn't have heard the house fall in. She must have been really something!'

There was only one way of cooling Jaime's lubricious interest – invention. 'She was.'

'Where did you find her?'

'Watching the return of the llaüts when a woman asked me if I spoke English.'

'What did she look like?'

'How can one describe Venus?'

'Who?'

'A flawless face framed with curling blonde hair; a figure to make one's hands tremble.'

'Go on.'

'We had a couple of drinks at the Bahia. Then we went for a walk along the beach and hadn't gone a hundred metres when she decided she wanted to swim.'

'So?'

'Couldn't be bothered to return to her hotel for a costume, so stripped off.' Alvarez paused. 'It was odd . . .'

'Her uppers?'

'No, how irritating sand can be.'

Sunday was Sunday even when there was work to be done. Alvarez did not have an early breakfast. As he ate the last piece of coca which Dolores had made, he considered a problem. Did he ring the mysterious Señor Riba from home, which would give him good reason not to rush to the post, or from the post and give the impression he had been working there since early morning?

He poured himself another cup of coffee since Dolores had not waited to be certain he had all he wanted. She was dusting the sitting room, having already cleaned the *entrada*; no visitor was ever going to think she did not keep her house immaculate. He added sugar and milk to the coffee. He would drive to the post before phoning. In the world of today, impressions were more important than facts.

Half an hour later, Alvarez settled behind his desk and dialled the number Dolores had given him. He introduced himself to the man who answered.

'I presume you were too busy to ring before?'

Uncertain to whom he was speaking – a senior member of the Cuerpo, of the Guardia Civil, a civilian who could cause trouble? – he answered politely. 'I have had to spend so much of my time on an investigation where every minute wasted may make the difference between success and failure that this is the first moment I have had free to call you back.'

'You'll not be wasting your time listening to me.'

A man who liked himself. 'Señor Riba, before we go any further, would you explain who you are?'

'Alexandro Riba of Riba y Hijo, detectives privado.'

Alvarez swore at himself for having bothered to be polite. Private detective – incompetent impersonation. 'So what have you to tell me? And please be as brief as possible because I am, as I mentioned, extremely busy.'

'My company, of which I am now head, following the retirement of my father some three years ago—'

'I am uninterested in the firm's history.'

'A pity. The story of many companies is a window into history. However, I feel you will not be interested in my thoughts on that subject.'

'Do you have reason for contacting me?'

'My phoning your office and on learning you were not there, asking for your home number and ringing twice, does not confirm that I do?'

It confirmed he was full of wind.

'Some three weeks ago, I was contacted by Señora Heron and—'

'Señora Heron who lived at Ca'n Ajo?'

'And is now dead. Yes.'

'Why did she come to you?'

'I am not wasting your time?'

Snarky bastard! 'Of course not.'

'The señora came to our offices and wanted her husband to be watched because she had reason to believe he was having an affair. She gave me the name of the lady concerned and wanted her husband watched every night to note if he visited the lady. I pointed out that such surveillance would be expensive, but she seemed careless about the cost and insisted it was to be carried out.'

'What is the woman's name and address?'

'Señora Hilary Rowley. English, of course. She lives in Cana Llagena, sin numero, along Cami de Gorriana.'

'Thank you for being in touch—'

'You are not interested in the rest of what I have to tell you?'

'I did not realize there was more.'

'Much more.'

Alvarez visualized Riba as short, bald, foxy-featured, maliciously inquisitive.

'One of my operators was off sick and I was having to do his fieldwork. I took up station outside Cana Llagena to the side of the house from where I could watch both front and back. At half past ten, my mobile rang; Señora Rowley had flown over in an earlier plane than her original booking and had arrived home to find her husband was not there. Was he with that bitch? – I use her words, not mine.

'I had to tell her he was at Cana Llagena, with the señora in one of the bedrooms.'

'How could you be certain of that?'

'Shutters appear to blank out a room because of the slant of the slats. But if one is immediately under a window and looking upwards, one can see between the slats into the room. You did not know that?'

'Never had occasion to.' Alvarez was not going to have Riba thinking the Cuerpo's work was ever reduced to spying on amorous couples.

'There seemed no reason at the time to add that they had, or very soon would, commit adultery.'

'Why so sure?'

'They were naked.'

'How did she react to what you did tell her?'

'Rang off. Even though she suspected, I believe she had still hoped she was wrong. Women are seldom capable of being realists where love is concerned.'

'What did you then do?'

'I remained where I was. Good surveillance lasts. Which is why, just after a quarter past eleven, I saw him leave Cana Llangena and walk in the direction of his own house. At ten past midnight, I had decided my work was completed and was about to walk to my car when I heard a shot.'

'Are you sure of that?'

'As certain as I can be without having seen the gun fired.'

'The sound was loud and clear?'

'To some extent muffled; nevertheless, identifiable.'

'From which direction did it come?'

'Ca'n Ajo.'

'Could the trees have confused sound and direction?'

'I leave others to decide that.'

Alvarez added a little Chaplin moustache to his mental picture of Riba. 'Was it one shot or two?'

'One.'

'There is evidence two were fired.'

'Then the first will have occurred when I was to the side of the house and the sound was shielded. When I left there, I circled the house and was in direct line with Ca'n Ajo. That, Inspector, is all I have to tell you. I hope I have been of some little assistance in your investigation.'

Alvarez muttered word of thanks, replaced the receiver. He was going to have to phone Palma yet again: Salas would find pleasure in reminding him of the character uplift he had given Heron. He opened the bottom right-hand drawer of the desk, brought out bottle and glass, poured a to-be-needed drink.

The brandy induced some optimism. It was Sunday. Salas would be on a golf course, proving he was no swinger.

His call was answered by the secretary with a plummy voice.

'You're back then. I hope you are better?'

'Thank you. Who is speaking?'

'Enrique Alvarez—'

'The superior chief does not welcome the use of Christian names. Where are you speaking from?'

She lacked any sense of humour or he would have replied, 'Hawaii.'

'Llueso.'

'The reason for your call?'

'To leave information for Señor Salas.'

'If it is important, you will give it to him now.'

'You're not saying he's there?' Wishful thinking had proved as useless as ever.

'Why should he not be?'

'It's Sunday.'

'The superior chief works to the job, not to the calendar.'

And his calendar contained no Sundays, no fiesta days . . .

'You were told to hang on, not go for a walk,' Salas said.

'It's Inspector Alvarez from Llueso—'

'You find it necessary constantly to remind me of that unfortunate fact when it is obvious from the moment you start to speak?'

Alvarez mentally sighed.

'What is it?'

'I have a fresh report to make on the Heron case, señor.'

'Then do so and stop wasting my time.'

'This morning, on arriving here early because of the pressure of work, the phone rang; the caller, Riba, is a private detective.'

'You have been employing him on the grounds he was more likely to conduct an efficient investigation than you?'

'He was employed by Señora Heron. He gave me some very interesting information.'

'To interest you, it must be of a carnal nature.'

'He was asked to confirm that her husband was having an affair.'

'Your interest is explained. It is very unfortunate, though not surprising, that I learn such an important fact from a private detective and not from my inspector, supposedly in charge of the investigation. You have questioned this woman and Heron to confirm the truth of the illicit relationship and to judge to what extent it provides the motive for the murder?'

'Not yet because—'

'To have done so would have shown initiative and enthusiasm?'

'I have only just received the report.'

'Small reason for the delay. You will immediately question them.'

'Señor Riba was able to give me further information.'

'Which you had failed to ascertain?'

'He saw Señor Heron leave Cana Llagena at a quarter past eleven on the night of the señora's death.'

'Not knowing where Cana Llagena is, the significance escapes me.'

'It is where Señora Rowley lives.'

'Would it be too exhausting to explain who she is?'

'The woman with whom the señor is having an affair.'

'A typical report from you! You provide information not gathered by you as it should have been, not in chronological order; and because of your penchant for lewdness, you assume that when a man visits a woman, his motive cannot be mere friendship.'

'They were in a bedroom.'

'Your mind immediately conjures up lustful thoughts.'

'They were naked.'

'How can this man know that?'

'If one gets under shutters and looks up through the slats—'

'You will question both—'

'Señor, I have not finished relating the evidence.'

'It is to be hoped it is not of the same nature as you have just provided.'

'Riba did not leave immediately after gaining the evidence he sought. Señor Heron left the house at a quarter past eleven. At ten past twelve, Riba heard a shot from the direction of Ca'n Ajo.'

'One shot or two?'

'One. I questioned him about that and it seems initially he was at the side of the house and so any sound from Ca'n Ajo would be masked. It was after he had moved to the back of the house that he heard the shot.'

'The sound was clear?'

'He described it as somewhat muffled; nevertheless, identifiable.'

'How far apart are the two houses?' Salas asked.

'I am not certain.'

'You have not thought to find out?'

'There hasn't been the time.'

'Do you ever find time to do your job? You will measure the distance now.'

'But the light is beginning to go.'

'There are werewolves around?'

'It will be difficult to judge the probable route the señor

would have taken, a route that may even be marked by use, when it is darkish. There is no street lighting.'

'You will determine the measurement as soon as possible and report it to me immediately.'

'If I do that at daybreak, señor, I will have to ring you at home. You wish to be awoken in the early morning?'

'Are you deliberately being more obtuse than usual? Or is that your mistaken idea of humour? As soon as possible means as soon as is practicable.'

The line went dead. Alvarez poured himself a second drink. Salas had been less aggressive than he had feared; was the bastard mellowing? In answer, the phone rang.

'Is that you, Alvarez?' Salas demanded.

Dare he ask Salas to whom he thought he would be speaking if he had dialled the office of Inspector Alvarez? Before he had time to decide, Salas spoke again.

'Are you incapable of answering?'

'Yes, señor.'

'Explain why.'

'Why what?'

'Why you are incapable, of course.'

'No, señor, not incapable.'

'You have just admitted that.'

'I was saying that yes, I am me.'

'Your reluctance to accept the fact is understandable; your grammar is not. Do you remember my initial comments on the case?'

'Not exactly.'

'When a man who is not rich is married to a woman who is, when he claims to have found her dead and it is clear she was murdered, when he provides an alibi which proves unsustainable, clearly he is the prime suspect.'

There was a pause.

'You have no comment, however absurd, to make? You expressed a belief he was not guilty, not because of a reasoned judgment based on evidence, but on instinct. Impressions were much more important than facts. Yet now we know Heron returned home shortly before a shot was heard and an hour and fifteen minutes before he reported her death.'

'He may have needed time to realize she was dead.'

'Was not his evidence that he found the outside door of the house unlocked, that fearing burglary, he checked downstairs then went upstairs and found her dead?'

'Yes.'

'Does instinct tell you why he did not report her death immediately?'

Alvarez did not try to answer.

'The most likely reason, based on fact – which is why it does not occur to you – is that he had to prepare the scene to make it appear to be a case of suicide and to calm himself for the inevitable interrogation.'

'Then why remove the gun?'

'Murderers are seldom intelligent.'

'Finding one's wife dead must be a terrible shock . . .'

'In some instances. You will question him again, demand permission to search the house thoroughly, examine his financial position; you will determine his relationship with this other woman; you will tell a cabo to fire a facsimile automatic in Ca'n Ajo to learn whether you hear the shot outside the woman's house. Clearly, wind can make a difference in audibility. Was it windy at midnight on Thursday?'

'I can't say off-hand.'

'Now that the question has occurred to you, you will find the answer. Have the safes been opened?'

'Not yet.'

'It was wishful thinking when you informed me you had arranged for them to be?'

'Orfida, the locksmith, is very busy.'

'You did not think to say it was priority?'

'I said it was very important.'

'You have checked the firearms records to make certain if Heron owned a gun with legal permission?'

'I was going to do so—'

'When you had the time? Have you organized the search for the gun?'

'I am in the progress of doing so.'

'Where is it most likely to be found?'

'There are a large number of flowerbeds and—'

'You don't think Heron might have more intelligence than to throw it into a flowerbed, one of the first places to be searched?'

'If he was frightened and distraught, as one would imagine a murderer to be, I don't think he would have considered what he was doing. The throwing of the gun would have been a gesture of repugnant self-condemnation.'

'He kills his wife and immediately suffers self-condemnation? He is devoid of any intelligence?'

'But if Heron was not the killer—'

'Does the property have a well?'

'I imagine so.'

'Imagination has no part to play. It either does or does not. Obviously this is yet one more fact you have failed to establish.'

'So much water is needed for a garden that size, it must have a well.'

'Water is bought and wasted by foreigners all the time. However, on the assumption that there is a well—'

'Señor?'

'What?'

'In the past, you have told me never to work on an assumption. Yet you've just said—'

'You will find out if there is a well and then search it to learn if the gun has been thrown down it.'

'That may be all but impossible.'

'Only to someone lacking any initiative.'

'The well may not have been cleaned out in years; there could be many centimetres, even metres, of mud; it may be fed directly from an underground stream, making it impossible to pump out. If it is lined with maress, that may have begun to crumble to the extent the well is dangerous.'

'You have further potential disasters to call upon to avoid the task?'

'Perhaps a large magnet would be better.'

'You understand the attractive forces of a magnet underwater?'

'No. But during World War Two, explosives were attached

to anchored ships by magnetism. And it may well have happened in World War One—'

'You intend to cite all past wars?'

'No, because magnets would have been useless when ships were made of wood. And even if their bottoms were sheathed in copper to avoid fouling, that is non-magnetic—'

'If you wish to discuss the build of quinqueremes, do so in your own time. Speak to Forensics; question Heron; search the grounds; find out if a shot fired from a handgun is inaudible from the far side of Señora Rowley's house; determine whether anyone else saw Heron make his way from one house to the other and how long it would take to do so; question Señora Rowley concerning her relationship with Heron; and, even though this requires some subtlety, learn whether she expects him to marry her now. I want the answers tomorrow morning.'

'But—'

'Well?'

'It is Sunday.'

'I am aware of that fact.'

'It may take even longer to carry out all your orders.'

'I would find that unusual?' Salas rang off.

Ten

It was market day. In the old square there were stalls with fruit, vegetables, herbs, sweets, cheeses; two large vans, with extended awnings, sold ice cream and *buñuelos* – deep-fried, thick straws of wheat, sugar, olive oil, grated orange skin and a taste of aniseed. For sale in the new square were clothing and accessories, shoes, kitchen and gardening equipment, mementoes.

Alvarez pushed his way through the hundreds of foreigners, bussed into Llueso, who had nothing to do but look, buy things they probably didn't need or want, eat and drink. In bitter contrast, he was faced with working all day and most of the night for the foreseeable future. The world was divided between those who could waste time and those who had no time to waste.

He entered Club Llueso and suffered grounds for further annoyance. With so many persons present, it was almost five minutes before Roca, the bartender, put in front of him the brandy he had not needed to order. 'That'll make you look a little less sour.'

'It might, if it were a decent measure,' Alvarez said, as he raised the glass and examined the depth of the contents.

'If the boss ever sees how much I pour you, I'll be fired.' Roca hurried along the bar to serve another impatient customer.

Alvarez picked up the glass and turned, intending to sit at one of the window seats; they were all occupied. He wondered if one couple imagined they were still at the beach. She wore a revealing, crocheted jacket over a mini bikini; he was bare chested.

Roca returned to face Alvarez. 'Now what's got you swearing?'

'Foreigners.'

'What's wrong with 'em so long as they're spending stupidly?'

'The way they dress is an insult.' Alvarez indicated the couple at the window table.

'I suppose he'd look less apish if he wore a shirt. But what's wrong with her? Upsets you because you can't be certain how much you're seeing?'

'You don't understand what I'm saying.'

'Doubt anyone ever does.'

'The old ladies of the village get very upset when they see foreigners dressed or undressed like that. It makes them think they're living somewhere which is no longer respectable. And it makes the local youngsters think it's smart to look half-dressed. Remember when women kept their virginity until they were married?'

'Do I look that ancient?'

'And if maybe one made a mistake, she had to marry in black at night?'

'Painful memories?'

'The young are beginning to look like *putas*. They're wearing their slacks and shorts so low at the back that much is visible.'

'You must be old and sad for that little valley to excite you. Maybe that's the problem. You've given up hope.'

Alvarez banged his empty glass on the bar. 'Are you still serving?'

Roca reached across to pick up the glass. 'It's a funny thing, but even a couple like them show more manners than some Mallorquins.'

'And an armless chimpanzee can serve customers more efficiently that most Mallorquin bartenders.'

Seated at a recently vacated window table, refilled glass in front of him, Alvarez thought about the future. Salas was demanding a week's work be completed in a day. But a complex investigation had to be conducted carefully, cautiously, exhaustively, leaving nothing undone, no small piece of evidence unappreciated. Rather than tear around as if he had sat on a palm thorn, he needed to move slowly, surely, consider carefully, let nothing distract his mind . . .

The bikini-clad lady and her companion stood. As she eased her way between the chairs of one table and those of the next, the movements of her body were visible through the jacket. She epitomized one of the sad ironies of life. Had she been twice as attractive and half the size, she would not have dressed like that.

He returned to the post, climbed the stairs slowly, thankfully settled behind the desk. Cautiously, carefully, exhaustively, he needed to examine the known facts of the case, the possible consequences of unknown ones, how best to continue the investigation . . .

He drifted into a comforting nap.

He phoned Ballistics soon after six.

'You want to know what?' demanded the man at the other end of the line.

'The make and type of gun that was used to kill Señora Heron and were the two shots fired from the same gun.'

'You know what day this is?'

'Of course.'

'Then you're a comedian. Try again tomorrow.'

'The superior chief—'

'Is not head of this department.'

'Hang on.'

'What the hell is it now?'

'Does Señor Heron hold a licence to own a handgun of any description?'

'Ask him.'

'Can't you check quickly?'

'What's the hurry? To find what's on the menu along the beach? All right, give me name and address and I'll look, being too generous for my own peace.'

Alvarez gave the information, waited.

'No, he doesn't.'

'You can be certain?'

The disconnected line was his answer.

He replaced the receiver. If he could not have the information about the type of gun until the next day, he could not organize the firing of one revolver in the bedroom at Ca'n Ajo. He fiddled with a pencil. He could question Heron. But the more time the other had to get over the terrible shock, the more likely his answers would be comprehensible and comprehensive. He could question the staff at Ca'n Ajo again, but they would be enjoying Sunday, their day off, and unlikely to be at the house; Ferrer certainly would not be working in the garden. He could question Señora Rowley, but she must be as mentally distressed as Heron . . . A man could only do what could be done. All he could do now was to return home.

Despite Dolores's cheerful mood, evidenced by the fact she had gone out early to buy the family *ensaimadas* and croissants for breakfast, despite the cloudless sky, for Alvarez, the day was grey. Mondays always were grey. There were five and a half working days before the weekend. Not that the past weekend had been one of relaxed pleasure.

'Are the *ensaimadas* not fresh?' Dolores asked.

'They're OK.'

'Then why have you not eaten the last of the ones I put out for you?'

'I'm not feeling hungry. The children will finish it.'

'Is something wrong?' Her concern was immediate.

'Not really.'

'What does that mean?'

'Salas is demanding an impossible amount of work.'

She poured herself a second cup of coffee, sat. 'Being a Madrileño, he thinks of no one but himself. Tell him you will not work yourself to death.'

'He might encourage that.'

'What absurdity are you saying?'

'If I died, I think he would probably regard himself a lucky man.'

'Then he is a monster.'

That was true. It was also true that no matter how grey the day, a man needed to maintain his strength. He ate the remaining *ensaimada*.

'Is there so very much for you to do today?' she asked.

'Persuade Forensics to do some work; make measurements; check statements; question dozens, including the girlfriend, who'll be in a terrible state.'

'Whose girlfriend?'

'Señor Heron's.'

'He has been committing adultery?'

'I suppose one could call it that.'

'You would not?'

He realized his incautious words meant her good mood was suddenly in the balance. For her, faithfulness was next to, even on a par with, godliness. It had always been the custom for there to be no guilt borne by a married man who indulged himself, but this was not the time to hark back to a more civilized past . . .

'No doubt, this woman whom you euphemistically call a girlfriend – a more accurate description is easily given – is much younger than was his wife?'

'I've no idea because I haven't met her yet.'

'He is rich?'

'Relatively speaking, almost certainly.'

'Then you can be sure she is very attractive to an older man who looks in a mirror and sees what he wishes, not what is there.'

She had given him a hard glance as if including him in her condemnation.

'One thing's for sure, she's a much nicer person than the señora was. Her staff thought her an old bitch and staff are usually good judges of those who employ them.'

'It matters not what she was like, she was his wife. He should have honoured his commitment to marriage.'

Honouring honour could make for a miserable life.

So could work. On his return to the post, there was a message on his desk. Orfida, the locksmith, would be arriving at Ca'n Ajo at 1100 hours. Just in time to interfere with his *merienda*.

Orfida looked like a weightlifter with a quirky beard. His fingers were long, shapely and imbued with magic. Ten minutes after beginning work, he opened the door of the safe in the dead woman's bedroom.

'That wasn't very secure,' Heron muttered.

Orfida spoke to Alvarez in rapid Mallorquin, confident he would not be understood by Heron. 'They're all the same. Take hours to do the job and you're a bloody marvel; take minutes and the lock can't be any good.'

'He's very upset.'

'Yeah? Do I send the bill direct to you or to Palma?'

'Palma. You'll get paid sooner.'

'Can't be soon enough with prices rising all the time.'

'Unlike salaries . . . Can you see your own way out?'

Orfida left, carrying a battered case. The safe was fairly full – half a dozen jewellery boxes, files, papers.

Alvarez spoke to Heron. 'Señor, I think I will take everything out. Then I should be grateful if you will judge if any jewellery is missing while I look through the files and papers.'

'You have to do that?'

'I am afraid so.'

'There may be some very personal matters.'

'I will read and then forget.'

'I . . . I can't understand what you're looking for.'

'Any reference, however brief, which might indicate why the señora was killed and who might be guilty.'

Heron spoke bitterly. 'There's no privacy in death.'

Alvarez was glad Heron had not witnessed Doctor Noguero's examination of the body. He carried the tooled-leather jewellery boxes across to the bed, wondered what was the value he had in his hands. How many times his annual salary? 'I'll take the files and papers downstairs. It will be much easier with a table to put them on.'

He carried the files, in different colours, and loose papers downstairs and into the dining room. He sat at the table, opened the red file. Receipts, kept in order and, where considered necessary, annotated with what had been bought. A tidy-minded woman.

The green file contained copies of letters which clearly had been considered of more than passing interest, together with copies of some of the letters she had sent. She had written to Riba a month previously. In terms more usually met in hard business circles, she accused Riba of over-charging her by listing too many hours of work. If he refused to give a reason she could accept, she would report him. None of the other letters or copies of letters proved to be of any consequence.

In the yellow file were statements from two banks. The size of her income made him silently whistle.

Heron entered, pulled out a chair, sat heavily. 'As far . . . as far as I can judge, none of the large pieces are missing. All the rings and brooches seem to be there, but there are too many to be certain . . . It was gut-wrenching, remembering when I had last seen her wear some of the pieces . . .' He trailed off into silence.

'I am deeply sorry to have had to ask you to do that, señor, but it was necessary. Have you put the jewellery into your safe?'

'No.'

'I would advise you to do so, along with such papers as you consider important after I have been through them all.'

'All right.'

Heron stared at the contents of the blue file, which had been pulled out on to the table.

'I need a drink. Will you have one?' he asked.

'Not for the moment, thank you,' Alvarez answered, surprising himself.

Heron left. Alvarez examined the many documents. The insurance on Ca'n Ajo and the contents thereof. One and a half pages of closely printed, small type was needed to list the circumstances under which the insurance became invalid. Insurers always tried to exclude those calamities the insurance was meant to cover. Alvarez found details of the trust fund of Aubrey James Oxley, set up under the terms of his will. Belinda Margaret Heron, niece of Aubrey James Oxley, was the sole beneficiary of the income of said trust during her lifetime; on her death, the trust was to end and the capital was to be distributed between two named persons.

Alvarez looked up as Heron returned. 'Your wife enjoyed a considerable income under the trust, señor,' he remarked.

'Her uncle made a fortune in the money markets. When young, he had sold fruit from a barrow.'

'Am I correct in understanding she only benefited from the income of the trust and had no interest in the capital?'

'Yes.'

'And you cannot benefit from it?'

'No.'

Hardly surprising, Alvarez thought, that Heron spoke with such bitterness. He continued to look through the papers.

There were three wills. The first, by date, apart from a few legacies, named her husband as sole beneficiary. The second left Ca'n Ajo to one named person, her jewellery to another, and the residue of her estate to her husband. Was this when she had first suspected her husband of having an affair? Both the wills had been legalized and were in English and Spanish. The third was handwritten and had not been witnessed so was invalid. In this her husband was not named. Was this when she had become certain of his infidelity and viciously determined to hit him as hard as she could?

There was a life insurance policy, clothed in imitation red seals, for the sum of £250,000. Insurance companies rushed to accept, hesitated to give; so there were two pages in small print which listed events which would invalidate the policy. She could not pilot a plane or a helicopter; race cars or boats; sky dive; paraglide; travel to countries which the Foreign Office held to be dangerous; take part in competitive sports of a violent nature; entertain any activity which was likely to endanger life . . . Living was an endangered occupation since it must end in death. Did that render the policy invalid? At the bottom of the final page was a single word, written in pencil. *Cancelled.*

Alvarez stood, carried the policy to where Heron sat. 'Is this writing your wife's, señor?'

Heron stared at it, finally answered, 'Yes.'

'The policy has been cancelled?'

'I don't know.'

'In her last valid will, your wife makes several considerable bequests to certain people and then leaves you the
remainder of her estate.'

'So she told me with great pleasure.'

'Why should that be?'

'She knew how little it meant.'

'She had no savings?'

'She had a large secured income and an appetite for
spending. She believed only the lumpen proletariat saved.'

'Señor,' Alvarez said, ' I can report that Señora Heron's
safe has been opened.'

There was a brief silence.

'Am I,' Salas asked, 'to be allowed to know if the contents
have proved to be of any consequence?'

'There was considerable jewellery, several files containing
various papers, like letters and receipts for purchases.'

'Was any jewellery missing?'

'Señor Heron says all the major pieces are there, thinks
the smaller ones are as well, but can't be certain since there
are so many.'

'Would a burglar take the small jewellery and leave the
large pieces?'

'It seems unlikely.'

'You can accept there was no theft. Have you learned
anything from the files?'

'Señora Heron was very wealthy in terms of income—'

'Then we have, as I have tried to make you appreciate
– without success – a husband who commits adultery when
married to a wealthy woman. Inevitably, salacious desire
drives him to get rid of his wife in order to enjoy her money
and his ignominious pleasures. A situation repeated time
and again.'

'It's not quite like that. Señora Heron's income came
from a trust fund and on her death the capital does not go
to her husband, but to two other people. Señor Heron is
left only the residue of her estate which apparently is very
little. There is a life insurance for two hundred and fifty
thousand pounds—'

'You find that very little, too small a sum to be considered a motive?'

'If he killed his wife to get his hands on the insurance
money, he lost any part of the very large income she enjoyed
and the house he lived in; at best, the insurance money
would not provide anything like so pleasurable a lifestyle.

'He would have to buy, more likely rent, a property, and
rents are very high. Most of the luxuries he had enjoyed
would now be beyond him. So, logically, he would not have
murdered her however great his dislike of her, because to
do so would leave him hard-up, not to mention the fear of
being caught. And there's one more fact which appears to
render her death so unwelcome to him. She had written on
the insurance policy "cancelled".'

'You have confirmed it was cancelled?'

'I intend to find out as soon as possible.'

'That was before you rang me.'

Eleven

Alvarez sat in his car and perspired freely, despite the opened front windows and the fan full on. Heaven was shade, cool showers and a frosted glass of brandy.

He managed to forget his discomforts and studied Cana Llagena. Smallish, two floors and not many roof levels. That and the two houses beyond, each with reasonable-sized garden, had been built fifteen or twenty years ago and would have cost only a tithe of what they were worth now. Men who had been clever enough to foresee the astonishing rises in house values had made fortunes; he remained able to afford only a reasonable amount of Fundador, less Soberano, and no Hors d'age. In a world where all were born equal, a few bestrode the narrow world like Colossi, the large majority could only dream of winning the lottery.

The garden of Cana Llagena suggested Señora Rowley was a necessity gardener. Beyond was a field, roughly a hectare in size, in which a dozen red sheep grazed. It was good to see them. They were an island breed which had almost become extinct because they were not considered commercially viable. Recently, some farmers had under-stood that to allow them to vanish from earth was an ecological crime and were saving the breed. He honoured men who worked to protect Mallorquin life.

Beyond the field, the belt of pine trees marked Ca'n Ajo. Even in a heat which left a man drained of energy, to walk from one house to the other could not take more than ten minutes. Time for Heron to have returned to Ca'n Ajo before the shot was heard by Riba.

Since he had established what he had come to confirm, was there any need actually to walk from here to there? Not really. But Salas had a habit of often finding out what truly had happened. He would have to walk. Within half a dozen paces he was sweating heavily; a dozen more and his throat was parched. No man should suffer in the cause of justice as he was suffering.

The walk took eight minutes and thirty seconds. His visual estimate had been correct, making his physical discomfort unnecessary and his future discomfort – the return – even more so. However, one should always take advantage of circumstances. Since he stood outside Ca'n Ajo, he would enjoy the air conditioning and the drink which would be offered.

He rang the bell. Teresa opened the door. 'You again! You're out of luck, the señor is not here.'

He had not intended to question Heron, but could now inform Salas that he had, but had been unable to. 'It's hotter than ever.'

'Cool enough in here since Eva turned the temperature lower because she didn't sleep too well.'

'I've had to walk from there.' He pointed vaguely.

She was not interested.

'I feel dehydrated.'

'Like a packet of soup?' She giggled.

'My throat's lined with sandpaper.'

'Would you like a drink, then?'

'That would save my life.'

'Eva's gone to the village, but I can make you some coffee. Unless you'd rather have iced water?'

The present generation might be better educated than earlier ones, but they lacked much. Still, a starving man did not refuse stale bread. 'Some coffee, please.'

Twenty minutes later, as he finished the second slice of the strawberry sponge Teresa had put on the table, he thought to ask, 'Does this place have a well?'

She sat at the opposite side of the table, playing with some crumbs on her plate. 'Has to, with all the water they use . . . Oh! Sounds like I'm forgetting again. I said "they", but she's dead.'

'I doubt the señora would be upset.'

'You didn't know her.'

'Didn't like her, did you?'

'Why should I? Doesn't matter what Eva says about being nice to the dead, she bitched all the time because nothing was ever right. Gave everyone a miserable life, the señor most of all.'

'It seems to worry you that she was unkind to him.'

'Not exactly worry, but . . . Well, it didn't seem right. I mean, like I said before, he always treated her as if she was nice to him.'

'You were going to tell me about the well.'

'Was I?'

'Where is it?'

'Back of the oleander hedge.'

'Is it deep?'

'Must be. According to someone, can't remember who, a diviner said it was fed by an underground river.'

It would be impossible to pump dry. Then where, how, did one find a large, powerful magnet? And that problem reminded him he had not yet organized a search of the grounds. 'There's something I've been meaning to ask you. Have you ever seen a gun in the house?' He noticed she began to finger the crumbs on her plate very much more rapidly.

'Why are you asking?'

'Because it's my job to do so.'

'You've been listening to Diego. He's a nasty old man, always causing trouble with that tongue of his.'

Diego was probably his age, which meant it was ridiculous to call him old. 'What's he been saying?'

'It doesn't matter.'

'Has he been suggesting he knows who killed the señora?'

She withdrew her hand from the plate, fidgeted with a button on her dress. She spoke defensively. 'Only someone like him could think that wild.'

'How wild?'

'Thinks the señor couldn't stand the señora's behaviour any longer. It's his stupidity. Like he votes for the communists because then everyone will be given a new car.'

'Yet it must have been difficult for the señor. According

to Diego Ferrer, he heard the señor and the señora having a row over money.'

'People always argue over money.'

'You're trying to convince yourself, aren't you?'

'What's that mean?'

'Convince yourself that the señor could never have murdered the señora. Since you like him and think him a good man, why do you have to convince yourself?'

'I don't.'

'I think you do. And why? Because you've seen a gun around the house.'

'No.' She looked down at the table.

'I have to know.'

'What's he been saying?'

'Who?'

'Diego.'

'Why do you ask?'

'Because he's been telling you filthy lies.'

'Why should he have lied to me?'

'He lies to everyone. Look at Eva. Her father was dying and she was so worried, she couldn't cook like usual. The señora told her if she didn't do better, she'd be sacked. Wasn't interested in Eva's troubles. So I told Eva, even if you and Diego look at something but never see the same thing, ask him for some of the garlic. That'll make your cooking perfect again and the bitch will have to stop threatening you. He said he couldn't give her any because it was all gone.'

'He was ordered by the señora to pull it up and throw it away since it made her ill because she was a witch, according to Heron.'

'And you believed him?'

'Not that she was a witch,' he said hastily.

'He dug up the garlic before the señor and señora moved here. She learned about that and wanted to know where it was and he said it had all been killed by blight. She believed him until she learned he was selling it at crazy prices – been growing it hidden under other plants in a bit of the garden she ignored. Never seen someone go on as she did;

shouted at him that if he didn't return everything he'd taken, he was sacked and she'd call the police.'

'Can't have worried him that much. The police probably wouldn't have been able to prove anything and good gardeners can get a job any time they want.'

'Wasn't like that. He'd been betting very heavily and owed plenty. He reckoned to get that money from selling the rest of the year's garlic. But if the police came along, he'd have lost all he had. That would have cost him time in hospital or the undertaker's.'

'So what happened?'

'Nothing. She died.'

'This was recent?'

'Of course it was.'

'Where does he keep the garlic?'

'Can't rightly say, but likely in the shed. Keeps that locked like there's gold inside or I'd have taken some for Eva when her father was dying.'

Alvarez made a point of looking into his cup.

'You'd like some more coffee?'

'I would. And is there another small slice of sponge?'

Several minutes later, he said, 'About the gun . . .'

'I don't know anything,' she said with nervous haste. 'Never seen one.'

'I think you have.'

'Doesn't matter what you think.'

'When I asked you about one, you became very uneasy.'

'I tell you—'

'Perhaps they weren't here and you were having a look around and saw it?'

'I've never stolen anything. That bitch used to leave money around to see if we'd take it. None of us touched it.'

A cynic might say that was more proof of prudence than honesty had the cynic not understood the innate honesty of Mallorquins. 'You'll just have been indulging in a little curiosity. Working in a big house, one's bound to become curious about the people who live so luxuriously. It's fun to look in places where one can't if they're around; that's human nature.' He ate the last piece of sponge. He drank the second cup of coffee. He waited.

'It's odd,' she finally said. She returned a strand of hair behind her ear. 'Like you know, they have – had – separate bedrooms.'

'It's an old English custom. Prevents a lady suffering too often.'

'I suppose that's why so many of 'em look constipated. I always made the beds, tidied up, dusted down and vacuumed. One day I was doing his room after they'd left for Palma and I . . . I . . .'

'Decided to have a little look around. Nothing to it. Happens all the time in the best houses.'

'I wasn't going to take anything.'

'Teresa, you don't have to keep telling me that. I know you'd never steal so much as a cent. Where was the gun?'

It was almost a minute before she said, 'In one of the drawers in the dressing room.'

'What did you do when you saw it?'

'Pulled a shirt over it and shut the drawer quick.'

Disturbed, perhaps scared. 'Can you describe the gun?'

'That's not easy.'

'Little is. How long was it?'

'Ten, twelve centimetres.'

'Did it look shiny?'

'More a kind of black with some shading.'

'What was the butt like?'

She thought for many seconds. 'It was ribbed and I think there was a different kind of ribbing above that.'

'Was there any writing on the barrel?'

'There was some, yes.'

'What did the back of the gun do?'

'It curved so a thick bit stuck out in a point.'

'Is there anything more about it you can remember?'

'I only looked very quick.'

'Small wonder. Don't worry, your memory works far better than mine. Was there any ammunition?'

She shook her head.

'You didn't see any or you didn't look?'

'I wasn't going to mess around with anything after seeing that.'

'Thank you for telling me this, Teresa.'

'You won't . . . if Eva learns . . .'

'I promise you she won't hear anything from me.' He checked the time. 'Do you expect the señor to be back soon?'

'Can't say.'

Then there would be small point in wasting time by waiting at the house. But before he returned home and had a delayed drink – she seemed sharp and intelligent, but had no social grace – before lunch, he must go up, with her, to Heron's bedroom.

They entered a room similar in size to the dead woman's, yet far more simply furnished. To the right was the dressing room; to the left, the bathroom.

The dressing room, a third of the size of the bedroom, had built-in cupboards and an oak chest-on-stand on which stood a table mirror that, as Alvarez had previously decided, looked more suited to her dressing room.

'Where was the gun?'

She pointed at the chest-on-stand. 'The . . . the second drawer.'

He drove home.

Twelve

'Now?' said the sargento in tones of disbelief.

'That's it.' Alvarez, telephone to his right ear, sat back in his chair with crossed feet up on the desk. 'Tell them to pay great attention to the search under the trees. There's probably a lot of debris – fallen pine needles, that sort of thing.'

'I've two men away ill.'

'Flu?' Alvarez asked with concern. Flu was potentially dangerous and highly contagious so contact with fellow officers would need to be kept to a minimum.

'Belly ache. Found some forgotten prawns at the back of one of their fridges and the silly sods ate them. Can't the search wait until tomorrow?'

'As far as I'm concerned, but the superior chief always wants things done yesterday.'

'When was she murdered?'

'Minutes after midnight, Thursday.'

'And the gun's been missing since then? Can't be in that much of a hurry, can he? Or maybe it's you who isn't.'

'I couldn't be working any harder than I am.'

'So I've heard.'

A snide use of ambiguity? 'I'll leave it in your hands. There's one more thing. The well's probably deep, but has to be searched.'

'So how does one do that? Hire a mermaid?'

'It likely won't pump dry to let you go through all the muck that's accumulated at the bottom, so the best bet would be a large magnet.'

'Where does one get hold of one of those?'

'I wouldn't know, but I don't suppose you'll have any trouble finding one.' He rang off before the arguments began.

Organization was the art of finding someone else to do the job . . .

He dialled Forensics. 'Inspector Alvarez, Llueso. I wondered if you'd any results on the Heron case?'

'Hang on.'

What would their next meal be? *Bacalao al ajoarriero*? A very basic dish, invented by muleteers to provide sustenance as they crossed the country, it had recently found favour in starred restaurants. When the salt cod, olive oil, garlic and eggs, overlaid by a tomato sauce which included onion, peppers, and fine sherry, was cooked by Dolores, it became a dish beyond five stars.

'Sorry about the delay, but I had to find the notes. The bullet in the head was too deformed to give much information; the one in the thigh was in sufficient shape for us to say the gun used was almost certainly a point three eight Colt automatic – that's nine millimetre as near as dammit. Despite the deformity, we can be certain both bullets were fired from the same gun.'

Alvarez thanked the other, rang off. It seemed probable the automatic seen by Teresa was the one which had killed the señora.

The phone rang. He answered.

'You are recovered?' Salas asked.

'Recovered from what, señor?'

'Whatever has prevented you from reporting to me.'

'I have been working so hard—'

'Keep your report factual.'

'Since last speaking to you, I have learned that Señor Heron probably was in possession of an automatic, despite his denials.'

'Would you explain what "probable possession" is?'

'Teresa was—'

'It would help to know the identity of whom you speak.'

'I thought you'd remember, señor.'

'I was trying to correct your ineptitude; I do not need to question my own memory.'

'She does the housework at Ca'n Ajo. She was looking through the drawers of the señor's dressing table—'

'Why?'

'Inquisitiveness. It's very common.'

'No doubt, here, that is so. In the rest of Spain, there is respect for another's property.'

'Perhaps in this case one should be grateful for her curiosity.'

'As an islander, your attitude does not surprise me; as a member of the Cuerpo, it shocks me.'

'But because she did have a look around, she saw the gun.'

'Results cannot justify means. In any case, she was no doubt looking for something she could purloin without being caught.'

'She's as honest as anyone.'

'Concerning those who live on this island, I can accept that.'

'I resent the inference, señor.'

'I have to remind you the incidence of theft here is greater than almost anywhere else in Spain?'

'Theft on tourists carried out by criminals from Eastern Europe. And it's no worse than other seaside resorts. Wouldn't surprise me if it's a lot better.'

'You alone would be unsurprised. I phoned in order to learn what, if any, progress has been made in the investigation into the murder of Señora Heron, not to listen to excuses for your inefficiency.'

'But it's you who said—'

'Make your report and do not prevaricate any longer.'

'I questioned Teresa. As I have indicated, she is of an inquisitive nature and one day, looking through some drawers in the señor's dressing room, she saw a gun. She knows nothing about handguns, but from her description there can be little doubt it was an automatic. This is consistent with the evidence.'

'What evidence?'

'According to Ballistics, the gun used to kill the señora was a point three eight Colt automatic.'

'Why has this not been reported earlier?'

'Because I only heard from them a few moments ago.'

'Did the same gun fire both bullets?'

'I was about to tell you that it did.'

'Have you searched the house for the gun?'

'Previously, yes, señor.'

'Have you questioned Heron about it?'

'Having only just been told . . .'

'Time enough.'

'Not if I was to line up the evidence and report it to you, señor.'

'You have forgotten it was I who phoned you? You will question him immediately. How reliable is this woman who saw the gun?'

'I would consider her sufficiently reliable to accept what she says without reservation.'

'Are you considering arresting Heron?'

'At the moment, there are too many imponderables. There is no hard evidence that the gun Teresa saw is the gun used to kill the señora. Of course, the possibility that it was not is low unless one supposes there were two assailants, one armed. The gun that was in the dressing room is missing, which supports the likelihood it was the one used, but there is no proof that it was. It was unregistered so who would know it was there but the señor, and perhaps the señora, and Teresa?

'Name the señor the murderer and there are many more problems than answers. He has been having an affair which he believed was hidden from his wife, but was not. When he returned from seeing Señora Rowley, was his wife still alive? Did she accuse him of having an affair and, being a woman described as bitchy, did she shout and call his female friend every foul name she could remember? Did he, losing all self-control, shoot her? Yet the evidence is that he never once began to treat his wife as she treated him. The staff judge him extremely unlikely ever to have willingly hurt her. A man who returns home and finds his wife has been murdered can be expected to be shocked, distraught, frantic. Señor Heron was all those things.

'If he did shoot her, why fire from a distance before closing to deliver the fatal shot? Surely he would have realized that for anyone but an expert, it is very difficult to fire a handgun from a distance and hit the intended target. On the other hand, if he has the experience and skill to shoot accurately, perhaps he was so mentally stressed that his aim was bad.

'As you have mentioned more than once, señor, it is the little incidents which often prove most important. Why, when the señor returned to the house, was the front door unlocked? It seems reasonable to assume it was his wife, returning early – he did not know that – who left the door unlocked. On the other hand, remembering the burglary, she might have re-locked it before going upstairs.

'If she had re-locked it, there is the problem of how did it become unlocked? I suggest one remembers the burglary, which was probably carried out by the known suspect, Cortes. Perhaps Cortes found the two safes, but through lack of expertise and equipment could not force them on his first visit. So he returned with a mate. Experienced thieves can move about a house unnoticed by people in it. So one man worked on the safes while Cortes wandered around, seeking anything worth taking. He found the gun in the drawer of the dressing room, pocketed it.

'Even those experienced make mistakes. Something was knocked over, waking the señora. Uncertain what had happened, probably suspecting a gust of wind – shutters were shut, but some windows were open – she got out of bed and left the bedroom. She saw Cortes and shouted at him instead of immediately returning to the bedroom, locking herself in, and phoning for help.

'He reached the bedroom when she was halfway to the phone. He brought the gun out of his pocket and fired, hitting her thigh. She collapsed. Certain she would be able to identify him, he shot a second time and killed her.

'The problem with this is, there is not a single piece of evidence to suggest the presence of two men. If Cortes had been searching, he would have left everything in a ransacked state. If he had not been searching, how could he have found the gun? Had he arrived armed, contrary to everything known about him?

'Are there other possible suspects? Señor Rowley? Did he suspect his wife was having an affair with Señor Heron? If so, surely he would have shot him, not Heron's wife? Since his wife was having an affair, did he decide in retribution to have an affair with Señora Heron and, knowing her husband was with his wife, enter Ca'n Ajo? Did she reject him and anger, humiliation, all the emotions of a cuckolded husband, persuaded him to attempt to rape her? Did she rush into the señor's bedroom and grab the gun? Did he try to take it from her and in the struggle, it went off, shooting her in the thigh? Realizing there was now only one way of escape from very serious criminal charges, did he kill her? Yet how would he have got into the house? Did his wife have a key, which he stole or had a copy made?

'Ferrer, gardener at Ca'n Ajo, has fallen foul of one of the local gambling bosses because of debts. He owes money he cannot pay and faces serious trouble. Did he break into the house, seeking something sufficiently valuable to free him from his debts? Far from expert at housebreaking, did he make so much noise that she awoke, discovered there was someone in the house, collected the gun and faced Ferrer?

'Knowing that if she held him captive until the police arrived there was no possibility of escaping a prison sentence, might he have thought to leave and claim she was making up the whole episode or misidentifying him? Yet because of her character, she used words which inflamed him and he tried to take the gun from her and escape. In the struggle, she was shot. But had he determined to steal, would he not have done so when he knew both she and the señor were out?

'Riba had reason to dislike the señora. She had written in emotive language and accused him of swindling her. A Mallorquin does not respond calmly to the accusation of committing fraud.

'Perhaps he arranged to meet her at Ca'n Ajo to explain his costs. The staff were not at work because the señora had given them the evening off, so he could have visited her unobserved. If she spoke as she had written, she must have enraged him to the point where he was all but incapable of knowing what he was doing. Did she get the gun to defend herself, he tried to take it from her and the inevitable happened?

'For the moment, señor, I cannot add to what I have just said.'

'For that, I am grateful. You advance facts, question they are facts; you suggest what might have happened, give reasons why it could not; you name suspects, explain why they cannot be suspected. Your report is a labyrinth without any magic ball of thread.'

'Thread, señor?'

'Being a Mallorquin, you will not understand the reference. It is clear that far from making progress in the case, you have introduced confusion.'

'A little more work may sort things out.'

'I cannot share your optimism. You have questioned Heron again?'

'Not yet.'

'Have you spoken to Señor and Señora Rowley?'

'There has not been the time to do so.'

'Can the gardener offer an alibi?'

'It has not been possible to talk to him.'

'Have you questioned Cortes?'

'I haven't had the chance.'

'Does the sound of a shot carry from one house to the other?'

'It has been difficult to organize the test because I have only just learned what type of gun needs to be fired.'

'I congratulate you, Alvarez. Not once have you had to use the same excuse for not having done what you should have.'

'I cannot do the impossible.'

'And find the possible very difficult.'

'I have organized a search of the grounds and well to find the gun, if it is there.'

'You would expect it to be found where it is not?' Salas replaced his receiver.

Alvarez stared glumly at the desk. Salas did not fire a man with the desire to work ever harder. He looked at his watch. Not yet time to leave for supper, but who would argue over a few minutes?

Thirteen

There were times when a man needed to find himself, to regain the certainty that it was good to be alive. Alvarez started the day's work by driving down to the port instead of to the office. The sky was cloudless, but the heat had not yet drawn every gram of energy out of one; the bay was at its most beautiful – deep blue, mirror-smooth water; a yacht with multi-coloured sails ghosting along as she sought the hint of a breeze; happy swimmers; the marshland, sweeping around part of the bay to provide open space that was a habitat for the wild animals and birds. There was little development because there were still those in power who valued the beauty of nature rather than little brown envelopes.

He sat at one of the tables set out on the pedestrianized road and drank the brandy slowly, not because it was of such quality, but there were times to let life glide slowly past. Yet inevitably came the time when one had to accept that man was not born to enjoy anything for long. He finished the brandy, paid, walked across to his car, which was parked on a solid yellow line and beneath a notice which threatened the towing away of any car parked there. He pressed the remote to open the driver's door of his car and was about to climb in when a man said, 'That's going to cost you fifty euros.'

He stood upright, turned, faced a policia. 'That joke has whiskers.'

'You may be Cuerpo, but you're parked in forbidden territory. If I was the sergeant, I'd have the car towed away with you standing there and owing a hundred euros.'

'If you were him, I'd ask how Raquel is?'

The policia was surprised. 'You're saying he's got himself an extra?'

'Not saying anything, but if you were married to his wife, wouldn't you be looking for relief?'

'Some of the lads have been wondering since he started smiling occasionally.'

Alvarez stepped into his car, shut the door. The policia was too deep in thought to notice his departure.

He drove through the port, past the many blocks of flats and the small houses once the homes of fishermen, to the first roundabout where another motorist's swerve to make the exit he wanted had Alvarez swearing and braking hard. A tourist in a rented car was a driver's nightmare.

Did he question Heron or Rowley? There was little to choose in the distance from where he was, but an interrogation of Heron was likely to be more prolonged.

A quarter of an hour later, he approached Cana Llagena, wondering if Señora Rowley would be blonde or brunette, Señor Rowley a typical blah-blah Englishman too well brought up on the playing fields of Eton to consider his wife might be two-timing him. He parked on the small gravel circle, which needed weeding, left his car, crossed to the raised porch, climbed the steps, knocked on the front door which had recently been oiled.

The door opened. 'Good morning.'

She had spoken in Mallorquin, which created a good impression; few English bothered to speak more than kitchen Spanish, far fewer even to try to speak Mallorquin.

'Señora Rowley, I am Inspector Alvarez of the Cuerpo General de Policia.' Her expression made it clear she was not nearly as conversant in Mallorquin as her greeting had suggested. He switched to English. 'I should like to have a word with your husband if that is convenient?'

Dolores, ever ready to misinterpret a man's interest in a woman, had confidently judged Señora Rowley would be young, slinkily beautiful, shapely and eager. She was not young, her features were pleasant, not eye-catching, her clothes obscured rather than revealed, she wore little or no make-up, her manner was reserved.

'You say you want to speak to my husband?'

'Yes, señora.'

'I'm afraid he died some time ago; soon after we came to live here.'

'I apologize most sincerely.' She had spoken calmly, yet there had been underlying sadness. He was at a loss as to how to proceed.

'Is there any way I can help?'

'Yes, señora. Perhaps I might ask you a question or two?'

'Would you like to come inside?'

The sitting room offered comfort, but no luxury. There was a fan, not air conditioning; the television set was tubed; the curtains were without pelmets; the carpet was broadloom and worn; the furniture, Ikean.

'Please sit. And can I offer you something to drink, or is it too early?'

It was odd how the English seemed to think there was a time before which one should not drink. Nevertheless, it seemed in order to observe this odd misconception. 'Thank you, señora, but I should like nothing.'

She settled on the settee. Her cotton frock was simply cut and brightly patterned, her sandals plain leather; her only jewellery, apart from a wedding ring, was a necklace of small red oval stones which he judged not to be of great value. Not a woman to cause a man to take the deep breath which fed the flame of his imagination; a woman whom a man was lucky to know once his dreams of busty blondes were over.

'I imagine you are going to ask me about Tony?'

He was surprised by the forthright question and the inferred admission.

'Perhaps you expected me to be reluctant to admit the relationship? I might have been, but Tony said there was no way in which we could continue to keep it secret and therefore it would be far more sensible to admit it.' She spoke forcefully. 'And I want to make it clear that he wasn't keeping it hidden for his own sake. Even though Belinda gave him such a bitter life, he wanted to save her from learning he had found happiness with me . . . You look disbelieving.'

'Not intentionally.'

'You must understand, I am telling you the truth. I don't have to guess what people are saying. So many of the local British criticize and malign that the moment they heard Belinda had been murdered, they'll have named Tony the murderer, although in their usual double-tongued manner, they'll swear they don't believe it . . . Please, please don't listen to them.'

'I can assure you I have no intention of doing so.'

'You mustn't believe he had anything to do with her death.'

'It is too early to suspect anyone. That is why I question those who might be able to help me.'

'You thought Stanley was alive. Were you ready to think him the possible murderer?'

'As I said, there is no suspect.'

'Why should Stanley have killed her?'

'I do not know.'

'You must have had a reason.'

'Señora, when there are troubled relationships, motive may take a long time to be understood.'

She spoke unevenly. 'Perhaps you have been thinking he might have been having an affair with her, even though she was so detestable – they say all cats are grey in the dark. Maybe you thought she had threatened to tell me what was happening, knowing how much that would hurt?'

'Let me say again, the only reason I am here now is because I need to talk to anyone who, without realizing it, may know some information which might help me.'

She spoke more calmly. 'I'm afraid I've been sounding rather stupid. But things have been so disturbing . . . I want you to understand that my marriage was very happy. When my husband died, my world was shattered.' She stared into the past for a while. 'We'd been friendly with Tony, despite his awful wife, and after Stanley's death, Tony offered me the comfort of friendship without any strings attached. It was I who eventually . . . Why am I telling you all this?'

'So that I understand what kind of a man Señor Heron is.'

'Will that make any difference?'

'Perhaps all the difference.'

She stood. 'It may be early, but I need a drink. Will you change your mind?'

'Without trouble, señora.'

'What would you like?'

'Coñac with just ice, please.'

She left the room, returned and handed him a generous brandy with several small ice cubes floating in it. She sat, sipped the Amontillado she had poured herself. She looked at him, then away. 'You said you want to understand what kind of a man Tony is. You sounded as if you meant that, not because you thought I might say something that . . .'

'I need to know him as he is, not as he might appear to be.'

A couple of minutes passed before she spoke again. 'He accepts people until they give him cause not to; even then he regards them with quiet amusement rather than dislike or hostility. He sees the sun, not the clouds . . .

'When Belinda and he moved here, he had retired early because she was so discontented with life in England. Then he lost much of his money through fraud and at about the same time, she inherited a very considerable income. One would have expected them to continue to live a pleasant life, but she used the money to humiliate him.'

'Why would she do that?'

'Because her background was so different from his. He is from old-time landowners; she was from a world of modern smart-alecks who made a pound wherever there was a pound to be made, regardless of how. She thought his friends were always trying to patronize her, which they weren't, because their social outlook and her interests were so different; she humiliated him to get her own back . . . Oh, Christ!'

'Señora?'

'What have I done?'

'Explained some of the circumstances of their lives.'

'And said she made his life such hell that he . . . that he . . .'

'Many husbands suffer their wives' unreasonable behaviour, but hardly any resort to murder to overcome the problem. Most find warm companionship elsewhere, which Señor Heron was lucky enough to do.'

'You can understand that whatever did happen, he is totally innocent?'

'I know you are certain he is.'

'Which doesn't mean a thing,' she said violently.

'On the contrary. It means he has never said or done anything to make you believe him capable of having killed his wife. That provides reason for believing in his innocence.'

'You mean that?'

'Yes.'

'You'll find the truth?'

At the moment, the truth was that Heron had become relatively poor, his wife had become wealthy, he had found a lover and must have dreamed of living the rest of his life with her . . .

Alvarez sat at his desk and stared at the phone for a long while before he dialled. When the connection to Palma was made, he named himself and his area, asked to speak to the superior chief.

'Wait.'

There was a long pause. He was grateful for this even though the bitter moment was simply delayed, not eradicated.

'Yes?' Salas demanded.

'Inspector Alvarez—'

'What do you want?'

'I have spoken to Señora Rowley. Her husband died a few years ago and so no longer can be considered a suspect.'

'It is heartening to learn you can appreciate that fact.'

'Since one cannot envisage Señora Rowley shooting anyone—'

'Why not?'

'The kind of person she is.'

'Yet more instinctive reasoning?'

'In one way, I suppose it is.'

'Then it can be ignored.'

'But if you meet her—'

'Which I have no intention of doing at the moment.' Salas cut the connection.

Alvarez relaxed. The phone rang and he resentfully lifted the receiver.

'The search has been completed.'

'What search?'

'Just woken up? The search of the grounds of Ca'n Ajo, of course. That is, with the exception of the garden shed, which was locked. There was no sign of the gardener to get it unlocked.'

'Did you find the gun?'

'No.'

'Then it wasn't down the well?'

'It's one of the old ones, metres wide and probably a hundred deep. No one offered to jump in and drown.'

'You didn't use a magnet?'

'No local source has anything big enough to pick up a gun.'

'Get on to Palma—'

'You'll have to do that. We've been told you've taken up too much of our time already. We may not have found a gun, but in a flowerbed by the front door, amongst the plants, there were two cartridge cases.'

'That's something. What have you done with them?'

'Left them where they are, of course, for you to deal with.'

'Are they nine-millimetre cases?'

'Probably.'

'I'll get over and collect them.'

'As soon as you like since we've left one chap there to make certain they're not touched.'

Alvarez thanked the other, rang off. Why had the ejected spent cartridges ended up in a flowerbed? Whatever the answer, they had to be recovered and sent to Forensics in the hopes they would offer some hard evidence. But since a policia was guarding them, nothing would be lost by his returning home and enjoying lunch.

'Have you been for a hike over the Tramuntana?' the policia grumbled.

'I was on my way here until something very important turned up,' Alvarez replied.

'I suppose it's better late than never, as the big-bellied girl said at her marriage.' The policia indicated the long, narrow flowerbed to the left of the front door. 'They're there; the first one some two metres along.'

'If you'll hang on a moment, you can take them with you and arrange to send them to Ballistics.'

'My shift ended an hour and a half ago and I'm hungry.'

Alvarez watched the policia cross to a motorcycle and ride off. People had become selfish, no longer ready to help.

The two cases were seven centimetres apart. The might have been thrown separately, but their closeness suggested they had been thrown together. Why were they there and not with the gun, which had been so securely hidden?

He crossed to his car and brought out two plastic exhibits bags. He returned to the flowerbed and used a pencil to lift up each case and drop it into a bag. As he placed the bags on the front seat of his car, Ferrer approached from the road on a Mobylette. Alvarez signalled to him to stop. For a moment it looked as if he would ignore the request, then he braked sharply enough to send up a small spray of gravel. 'What is it this time?' he called out.

'The chaps who were searching the grounds couldn't get into the garden shed because it was locked. You can unlock it.'

'Tomorrow.'

'Now.'

'I've got to get the wife to the medical centre.'

'So why come back here?'

Ferrer did not answer.

'If you're off again, you can give me the key.'

'I look that stupid?' He turned the mobylette, began to accelerate.

'Hold it.'

He let the revs die down.

'When did you last weed that?' Alvarez pointed at the flowerbed by the side of the front door.

'What business is it of yours?'

'Until I know who killed the señora, everything is my business.'

'Well this ain't everything.' Ferrer drove back to the road.

Alvarez watched him until he was out of sight. He was full of tongue – more bluster than bite? Like most Mallorquins, he was probably very quick to anger and full of arrogant pride, so when he was called a thief . . .

Alvarez sighed. He opened the driver's door and was about to climb in, when he checked the movement. With Ferrer away, he had the chance to examine the garden shed.

Ferrer must regard that as a safe hiding place.

The wooden building was roughly four metres long, two wide, and was windowless; the door was secured with a large padlock of relatively simple construction so that a couple of minutes and a small metal tool which resembled a toothpick, given to him by a man when arrested, opened it.

The hut contained a great number of gardening tools, hosepipes, sprayers, electric mower and hedge cutter, collapsible steps, tins and spray cans of this and that and a filled sack. A quick search showed that if the gun was hidden in the shed, it must be in the sack. The faint aroma had told him what was inside this before he opened it.

He reached down into the cloves of garlic and, with difficulty, moved his hand around. No gun. He withdrew his hand and in the palm was a single clove. Escoffier would have sold his soul for that; the Cullen diamonds glistened no more brilliantly; gold was not as valuable.

The greatest gift a man could offer was happiness. Given the one clove in his hand, Dolores's happiness would, for a time, be complete; she would not concern herself with what he and Jaime drank, would not complain about the lot of women, her cooking would reach fresh pinnacles of excellence . . .

But to take one tooth out of one clove would be theft. It mattered not that its disappearance could harm no one, would not even be remarked. He dropped the clove back into the sack.

'Now what made me reckon you might be here?'

He turned to face Ferrer, who stood in the doorway with an expression of sneering satisfaction.

'Helping yourself as hard as you can go?'

'I have helped myself to nothing.'

'It wasn't garlic in your hand?'

'If you saw that, you also saw me drop it back into the sack.'

'Only because you heard me.'

'I did not hear you. And no matter what, the clove would have been returned.'

'I suppose you opened the sack just to have a look?'

'To search for the gun.'

'When you first came, you couldn't stop talking about the garlic and hinting you'd like some; every time you've been here since, it's the same. Tried everything to get me to give you some, so when I wouldn't, you fiddled the padlock and broke in. If I hadn't been suspicious, you'd have filled your pockets.'

'I would not have taken anything.'

'People will believe that when I tell 'em I saw you with a clove in your hand and the sack wide open?'

The circumstances could be thought incriminating by someone who wished him ill. A whispered word was often trusted more closely than a spoken one. Was Ferrer threatening him in the hopes that by doing so, his part in the murder was less likely to be uncovered?

'That garlic is worth an arm and a leg,' Alvarez remarked.

'Think I don't know that?'

'Your arm and your leg.'

'What's that supposed to mean?'

'You're hoping it will make you enough money to pay off your gambling debts and so avoid physical encouragement to pay up.'

'Who's been saying them lies? Someone in the house?'

'A whisper in the streets.'

'I ain't got no debts.'

'Then that's welcome news for you since I am going to take the sack of garlic with me.'

'You bleeding well don't!'

'It was grown on this land and you were paid to grow it so it belongs to the landowner. It will have to be determined when this crop was sown and harvested, who owned the house on each occasion, before we know from whom you intended to steal it.'

'She gave it me.'

'Señora Heron did? After she had accused you of stealing it?'

'She didn't understand.'

'What?'

'The custom.'

'Which one?'

'That when a man grows for someone else, he has a little of what's harvested.'

'What is a little in this instance? A dozen cloves? I'll give you a dozen and tradition will be satisfied. The remainder goes to the post and the law will be satisfied.'

'You ain't the right.'

'You can argue your case in court.'

'But I—' He stopped abruptly.

'You're worried that it'll all take time. It will. And you haven't the time in which to find the money to pay off your gambling debts, so you'll be meeting the enforcers. All you can hope is that they're not so enthusiastic that they leave you totally disabled.'

'But . . .'

Alvarez waited.

'Couldn't you . . . Look, when I said what I did about you and the garlic, I was joking.'

'You should be more careful with your jokes.'

'Straight, it was just talk.'

'Talk causes most of the troubles in the world.'

'I swear I wouldn't have said anything to anyone.'

'Good to know. How much do you still owe?'

'What's it to you? . . . All right, two hundred and fifty euros.'

'Would you get that much for what's in this sack?'

'If I didn't keep any back.'

'Why should you?'

'For next season's planting.'

'You'd sell that?'

Ferrer looked at Alvarez, uneasy at the other's hard tone. 'I've got to find the money.'

'You would condemn this miracle of nature to extinction just to save your miserable self?'

'They could leave me crippled.'

'Too soft a fate for a man guilty of the crime of the millennium.'

'They've got to be paid.'

'Take out the cloves you need for next season and store them very, very safely.'

'But—'

'Now! Unless you want me to start the enforcing?'

'But then there won't be enough left.'

'You're keeping back a full crop for next year.'

Ferrer was desperate. 'But they'll maybe even kill me.'

'So you'll pay what you owe.'

'How can I if I don't have enough money from the selling?'

'I'll give it to you.'

'You . . . you'll help me?'

'I'm concerned with preserving a miracle, not with you. I give you the two hundred and fifty, you repay me regularly or you'll be in even worse trouble than you are now.'

'What will you do with the garlic?'

'Take it to the post where it will be held until it's decided who's the rightful owner; that is, after you've collected up enough seed garlic and make certain it's in prime condition.'

Thirty-five minutes later, Alvarez checked his credit in the telebanco outside Sa Nostra. 262 euros. He withdrew 250, handed the four fifty-, two twenty- and one ten-euro notes to Ferrer, who expressed his thanks with sycophantic excess. He was left with twelve euros until next pay day. He would have to delay the monthly payment he gave Dolores to pay his share of the housekeeping, make few visits to cafés, smoke only Ducados. Sacrifices made for the benefit of all humanity. Yet he failed to enjoy the warm glow of exaltation such a sacrifice was meant to bestow.

He drove to the post, switched off the engine, stared at the sack on the front passenger seat. In one sense he could say he had bought the garlic since he had paid for it. But then it had not been Ferrer's to sell. Indeed, for the moment it was impossible to say who was the true owner . . .

Part of the truth of a country is often to be found in its customs. Ferrer had been right to claim that island custom had in the past allowed him, as an employee, a proportion – a small proportion – of the crop he had grown. Therefore, custom allowed that some of the garlic was his. Then surely, he, Alvarez, had paid for that proportion? But he had demanded repayment of the money. Yet he had not asked for interest and therefore who could deny that he had paid for a small proportion of Ferrer's small customary share?

Alvarez passed through the *entrada*, as immaculately clean and tidy as ever, and in to the dining/sitting room. Juan and Isabel were arguing as they watched the television, Jaime sat at the table, his expression mournful, an empty bottle and glass in front of him.

'So how are things?' Alvarez asked, as he sat down opposite Jaime.

'Bloody awful.' He pointed at the kitchen doorway to indicate Dolores was in one of her odd moods. As if in response, she came through the bead curtain.

'Are you unable to speak as does a decent man?' she demanded, staring at her husband.

'What's that about?'

'You are careless that your speech is that of a vagabond?'

The children had ceased arguing and were listening with interest. 'What's a vagabond?' Isabel asked.

'Someone whose tongue speaks from the gutter, who

cares so little about his wife's comfort that he refuses to mend the fan in the kitchen, even though it is so hot in there that the fires of hell would be cooling.'

'I said I'd see what I could do about it,' Jaime protested.

'Many times over many years.'

'That's talking daft.'

'You cannot face the truth? And better daft than disgusting.'

'Are you saying I've been talking disgustingly?'

'You do so so often, you are no longer aware of the fact?'

'What have I said to disgust you?'

'I did not say I was disgusted – one can become accustomed to almost anything if one has to suffer it long enough. But to swear in front of your innocent children is disgusting.'

'When have I sworn in front of them?'

'When you replied to Enrique after he asked you how things were.'

'All I said was—'

'You will not say it again.'

'I know worse words than that,' Juan said proudly.

'Of course,' Dolores said sharply. 'When a father is unable to speak politely since he has learned his words in the gutter, his children inevitably become acquainted with them. However, if they believe it is clever to repeat them, they very soon learn their error.' She regarded each of them in turn, went back into the kitchen.

As the children resumed their arguing, Jaime leaned forward and spoke quietly. 'She's been like that since I got back.'

'What's upset her this time?' Alvarez asked.

'How can I ever tell what starts her off? Some kind of woman trouble, maybe. They suffer so many, a man can't keep up with them.'

'And what are you doing sitting in front of an empty bottle and glass?'

'There was only a sip left and there's nothing in the sideboard. If she bought any coñac and wine this morning, she hasn't said.'

'Then someone needs to ask her.' Alvarez stood.

'Best leave her alone or she'll get really sharp.'

'I doubt that.'

'Of course she bloody will—' Jaime hurriedly stopped.

'Do you think Mummy heard you?' Isabel asked sweetly.

'I didn't say anything.'

'Yes, you did, and she'd like to know about it.'

'There's no need to disturb her when she's cooking. Just forget it.'

'Why?'

'Because if you're not careful none of us will get anything to eat.'

Alvarez walked into the kitchen.

'What do you want?' was Dolores's sharp greeting.

'There doesn't appear to be any coñac or wine.'

'I am expected to consider only your needs? Being a man, you assume I have nothing else to occupy myself. Beds make themselves, rooms tidy and clean themselves, food cooks itself.'

'I know you work really hard because—'

'Because I want my family to sleep in a clean house and to eat wholesome food. Of course, I realize how little my labours are appreciated.'

'They are greatly appreciated—'

'As my mother observed, a man's lips soften when he wants something.'

'And to show how greatly appreciated, I've bought you a small present.'

'Some other time. If the meal isn't on the table when you men think it should be, you complain bitterly, with never a thought to me, having to slave in here.'

He brought two cloves of garlic out of his pocket and showed them to her.

'Put them with the rest in the vegetable rack and then get out of here and leave me to prepare the meal.'

'You are not interested to know where they came from?'

'As if I have time to waste.'

'I have been working at Ca'n Ajo this morning.'

'And I have been working here since—' She stopped. 'Ca'n Ajo?'

'Yes.'

'And that garlic in your hand . . .?'

'Planted and grown there.'

'It is for me?'

'A small token of thanks from all of us.'

She stepped forward and took the two cloves from him. 'That a man should bring such treasure!' She kissed him on each cheek. 'With that garlic I will cook you a *carne de cordero provenzal* that will make the saints long to return to earth.'

'By the way, is there any coñac or wine out here?'

'Go back and rest after your hard day's work and I will bring it to you.'

Alvarez returned to the dining room.

'No luck, then,' Jaime said, seeing Alvarez's empty hands. 'Didn't I tell you?'

'What did you tell Uncle Enrique?' Isabel asked.

'You are not to listen to other people's conversations.'

'How can I help doing it when you speak so loudly?'

'If you want to chatter and not watch the television, switch it off.'

'Why can't I do both?'

'Because you cannot do two things at once.'

'I can breathe, I can see, I can hear and I can talk. That's four things.'

Jaime was about to speak when Dolores began to sing in the kitchen. He listened intently, gloomily certain that in her present mood, the song would be about man's duplicity, foretelling her mood would only darken.

She sang well and clearly. Pascual had known Natalia from their first day at school. Through the years, they had played together and lived in each other's home. One day, as they sat and watched some lambs in a field, Natalia had realized that for her, friendship had become love. How she longed for him to say it was the same for him. Yet he went out with her, laughed with her, held her hand, but treated her as a sister, not a lover. She would lie sleepless in bed, sadly convinced he would never speak the words she so desperately wanted to hear . . .

'The bastard's going off with someone else,' Jaime muttered.

'What's a bastard?' Isabel asked.

'Basket.'

'You said—'

'Basket.'

Isabel looked doubtful, but did not argue.

The song had reached a summer evening when they had walked past a field of corn and Natalia had tripped. Pascual had caught hold of her, looked down at her upturned face and confessed his burning love for her. The song ended.

Dolores came through from the kitchen and put a bottle of Soberano, a bottle of Sangre de Toro and a small bowl of ice cubes on the table. 'If I've forgotten anything, give me a shout.' She returned through the bead curtain.

Jaime stared at Alvarez. 'What the hell's worked that miracle?'

'A few sweet words never fail to sweeten.' He reached down to bring a glass out of the sideboard.

'Well?' said Salas curtly over the phone the next morning.

'I have a report to make,' Alvarez answered.

'You made it yesterday.'

'A fresh one.'

'You astonish me.'

'I have been talking to Ferrer, the gardener at Ca'n Ajo. He was considered a suspect because he had been accused by the señora of theft and to a Mallorquin such an accusation might well have led to her murder. Not that Ferrer would see it as murder.'

'More a friendly gesture? When national laws are considered to cease to have any meaning beyond the shores of the Peninsula, I suppose that is not surprising.'

'Is a man's character and reputation not important to him in Madrid?'

'A ridiculous and insulting question.'

'It is equally the same here.'

'Nothing is the same in Mallorca. Do you have anything of the slightest importance to tell me?'

'In my opinion, we need no longer consider Ferrer a suspect.'

'Why not?'

'He is incapable of committing any crime which calls for mental strength, steady nerves and an acceptance of the possible consequences of his act.'

'This profound judgment is based on what?'

'I have talked to him.'

'And he has given you a valid alibi?'

'No. I could judge he was no murderer.'

'You talk to a man and immediately understand who he is and of what he is not capable?'

'One can make a solid judgment when one watches how he acts under mental strain, señor.'

'Beyond your solid judgment – some might think thick would be a better adjective – is there any proof he did not murder the señora?'

'It is always difficult to prove a negative.'

'I have become convinced you find even greater difficulty in proving anything positive. Until there is a genuine reason not to do so, you will continue to regard him as a suspect. Have you questioned Heron again?'

'No, because—'

'Have you confirmed whether the sound of the first shot would have been heard by Riba?'

'There is some trouble—'

'Of your making, no doubt. Have you questioned Cortes to determine whether he robbed Heron's house and may have broken into it a second time?'

'Not yet.'

'Then I imagine you will not have spoken to the staff again?'

'I had that long talk with Ferrer—'

'Whom you had named a strong suspect since he had been called a liar by the señora, but who now, thanks to your acute psychoanalysis of his character, can be freed of any suspicion. From now on, you will remember you are a detective and will judge only on provable evidence. Is that clear, or do I need to repeat it in simpler terms?'

'It is quite clear, señor.'

'Would that I could accept your assurance with any confidence.' Salas rang off.

Fourteen

Teresa said the señor was at home and having something to eat and drink, so for the moment he could leave the poor man in peace. When he entered the kitchen, Eva's greeting was more friendly. Would he like coffee and one or two of the croissants she had just made – much nicer than the ones in the shops – perhaps with butter and jam? He ate three to confirm her judgment of her own cooking.

Teresa, who had left the kitchen a moment before, returned with a tray on which were two plates, cup and saucer, milk jug and sugar basin. 'He's eaten everything,' she said, as she put the tray down on the table.

'Hardly surprising,' Alvarez said.

'But last time Eva again cooked one of his favourite dishes and he hardly touched it.' Teresa sat. 'I've told him you're here.'

'How did he receive the news?'

'Never said anything.'

He finished his coffee, stood.

'Be kind,' Eva said. 'He's been suffering something terrible.'

'I'll be as easy as I can.'

'It's odd, really, seeing him suffer like he is when she wasn't worth a single tear.'

'Perhaps they were happier together than it seemed.'

'There's not a man could be with the likes of her. Still, there's some as like being unhappy.'

'There can't be anyone that stupid,' Teresa said.

'You've still a lot to learn. As you'll find out if you go on seeing that man of yours.'

'Why are you always making nasty remarks about Eduardo?'

'Because you're too good for the likes of him.'

'You think I don't know what I'm doing?'

'I'm hoping you ain't doing it.'

Alvarez intervened. 'Where is the señor?'

'In the sitting room.'

He left, certain the merits and demerits of Eduardo would continue to be discussed. Women could have very different opinions of the same man. Jealousy played a large part in that.

Heron stood as Alvarez entered. Far more composed, some of the evidence of strain had left his face. He held out his hand. 'Good morning, Inspector. They told me you were here and wanted a word. But first, may I offer you coffee?'

'Thank you, señor, I have had some.'

They settled in two of the armchairs.

'More questions?' Heron asked lightly.

'I fear so. You told me you returned home on the Thursday after having been down in the port at Café Pascual. That was not correct, was it?'

'No.'

'You returned here having been in the company of Señora Rowley.'

'And didn't admit that because I wanted to keep her out of the picture.'

'That is understandable, but it would have been much better if you had spoken the truth because now I wonder what other lies you have told me.'

'Everything else has been the plain truth.'

'You returned here Thursday night, found the front door unlocked, feared you had been burgled again, searched the house and tragically found your wife had been shot?'

'Yes.'

'No gun was visible?'

'No.'

'How long does it take you to walk to Cana Llagena?'

'I . . . I'm not sure.'

The first signs of uneasiness. 'You must have some idea. Five minutes, ten minutes?'

'Somewhere between the two, I guess.'

'Your car was here and you intended to drive to the airport to meet your wife, thinking she would be returning in the early morning, having been unable to book a more social flight?'

'Yes.'

'In fact, she managed to get an earlier flight. Why do you suppose she had not phoned you from England to tell you she would be arriving earlier than expected – the day before, in fact – so that she could be certain you would meet her?'

'I've answered these questions before.'

'Indeed. And I'm sorry to have to repeat them, but I have to make sure of something. You left Cana Llagena at seventeen minutes past eleven.'

'I don't know what the time was.'

'You were timed by a private detective.'

'A what?'

'You were not aware that your wife had hired a private detective to confirm you were having an affair with Señora Rowley?'

'Of course I wasn't.'

'You would have arrived here at around twenty-seven minutes past eleven. Would you agree?'

'I've no idea when.'

'The walk between the houses takes roughly eight to ten minutes. At ten past midnight, the private detective heard a shot; in his judgment, that was fired in this house. The times suggest you would have been here.'

'That . . . that's ridiculous. Belinda was dead when I got here.'

'Do you own a gun?'

'No.'

'Have you ever owned one since you have lived in this house?'

'No.'

'Señor, if you are to help yourself, you must speak the truth.'

'Damn it, that's what I'm doing.'

'A gun has been seen in your possession.'

'Impossible.'

'It was in a drawer in your dressing room.'

'Who's told you that lie? One of the staff?'

Alvarez did not answer.

'Was it Teresa who's so damned inquisitive?'

'The description given of the gun was not sufficiently detailed to identify the make, but that was determined by Ballistics as a point three eight Colt automatic. Knowing that, I am reasonably satisfied from the description that it was a Colt automatic in your drawer.'

'God knows why, but your informant is talking nonsense to harm me.'

'It seems very unlikely. The staff clearly have too great a regard for the way in which you have treated them to want to harm you.

'I have found two empty cartridge cases in the garden beyond the front door. These will have been the two cases ejected by the automatic. An intruder would pick up these cases because it is well recognized they can provide a gun expert with valuable information, but he would not have thrown them into the garden. Did you pick up the cases from the floor of the bedroom, too mentally disturbed to realize what you were doing, and then throw them into the garden in a gesture of rejection of what had happened?'

'You . . . you are accusing me of killing her.'

'I am trying to discover what happened that night.'

'She was killed. I found her dead. Yet you think I killed her.'

'Did you shoot your wife?'

Heron made a sound, part moan, part cry, stood and rushed out of the room. Alvarez stared at the far wall, his mind in a jumble. He had believed on good grounds – at least in his own mind – that Heron had not murdered his wife. He still wanted to believe that, not because he refused to accept he could be wrong – that often happened – but he still judged Heron to be too . . . humanely civilized was all he could think of – to murder his wife, however much provoked;

too intelligent to shoot her in the mistaken belief this would be to his financial advantage.

Heron returned. 'I . . . I had to move. My mind seemed about to explode. To be asked if I'd murdered Belinda, to blast her head apart . . .'

'There are times, señor, when my job can be very cruel both to someone else and to myself.'

'I did not, did not kill her. I swear to God that is the truth.'

'I take great note of what you say . . . By the way, is this yours?' He handed Heron a crude metal case for holding a pack of cigarettes.

Heron briefly examined it, returned it. 'No.'

Alvarez shrugged, pocketed the case. 'One thing I have to do is find out whether your wife's insurance was indeed cancelled, as she had written. Would you allow me to return to her bedroom and look at the folder to check the insurer's name?'

'I have transferred everything to my safe as you suggested.'

'Then if you'd open that for me . . .

Alvarez sat at his desk and wished he was a tourist on the beach with nothing more complicated to worry about than whether to dine at Restaurante Alhambra, whose speciality was *chuletas de cordero en salsa*, or Restaurante San Antoni, which was noted for *conejo con pimientos verdes*. He sighed. Wishes were but deceiving phantoms.

He phoned Doctor Noguero. An imperious woman – shades of Salas's secretary – told him the doctor was not available except by appointment. She was annoyed when he used his rank to ask to speak to him immediately.

'Yes, Inspector?' Noguero asked.

'You remember examining Señora Heron's body after she was shot?'

'Of course.'

'You gave an estimate of the time of death to be from three to four hours previously. Would a period of two and a half hours be too little?'

'I need to refer to my notes. Hold on, please. I'll be as quick as I can.'

Alvarez waited.

'Two and a half hours is outside my best estimate of time of death. However, as I explained, such an estimate can never be free of error because of the many imponderables, especially the heat. I would perhaps find it a shade surprising, but certainly far from impossible, that death was only two and a half hours before I made my examination.'

He thanked Noguero, replaced the receiver. He phoned the Policia Local in the port and asked them to give him Cortes's present address.

He settled back in the chair, satisfied he had done all that was possible for the moment. Gradually, he was beginning to bring together the pieces of evidence and . . . and what? Was Salas correct and he should not allow instinct even a whisper? Kindness and brutality could be the two sides of one character and to think one must disqualify the other was wrong.

The world began to dissolve as he remembered he had not done all that was possible; he had not spoken to the insurance company or arranged the firing of the gun in the bedroom of Ca'n Ajo . . .

The world dissolved.

The brigada was in a morose mood. He enjoyed a good salary, but his wife seemed to think he earned twice as much. She had a passion for shoes – a common failing in women – and had just bought a ridiculous skeleton-like pair in Palma for so many euros he tried not to remember how many and in consequence they haunted his mind.

'Yes?' he said aggressively, when Alvarez entered his room on the ground floor of the post.

'I need help.'

'So I keep hearing.'

Alvarez ignored the inference. 'I have to arrange for a gun to be fired so that I can check how the sound of the shot carries.'

The brigada examined his fingernails to make certain they were smoothly filed.

'So if you'll arrange for a cabo to stand by to help . . .'
'When?'
'As soon as he can lay his hands on a point three eight Colt automatic.'
'And where is he supposed to find that?'
'Not my department.'

It was a not-quite time. Not early enough to begin new work, not late enough to be seen to end work.

The phone rang. Unwillingly, Alvarez reached out and lifted the receiver.

'Policia Local. You were asking for the address of Domingo Cortes.'

'Have you had any luck?'

'We rely on work, unlike you blokes.' The policia chuckled. 'Fifteen, Carrer Aragon, Mestara.'

He used the back of an envelope to write down the address. 'What can you tell me about him?'

'Busy small-time thief. Been inside five years back, but since then has sharpened his act and not been caught. We were certain he did the job at Ca'n Ajo, yet none of the stolen goods have surfaced and we've never been able to prove it was his work.'

'Is he normally armed?'

'Slides and slithers, not fights, his way out of trouble.'

'Is there any record of his working with others?'

'He's a loner.'

'I've been wondering if he might have teamed up with a peterman?'

'Very unlikely. He'd see it as too much of a risk to do a big job and no smart safebreaker would want to have to rely on him.'

'What made you suspect him of the Ajo job?'

'He's invented some sort of gadget which opens closed shutters. It's unique as far as we know and our only proof that it exists are the marks left on the shutters – two indentations in the wood near the locking bar. Those two marks were on one of the shutters of the main downstairs room. Without the gadget that made them, they proved nothing.'

Alvarez thanked the other, rang off. It was now too late to question Cortes; but soon it would not be too early to leave for home.

The phone rang after he had left the room and started to descend the stairs. He came to a stop, left hand on the banister. To return or not to return, that was the question. The call might be from Palma. Salas was fool enough to work extra hours, forgoing one of the cherished benefits of high office.

He returned upstairs.

'I've tried to ring you several times,' said the superior chief's secretary in her most magisterial tones.

'It's only rung here the once and I would have answered it before, but I was halfway down the stairs – to go and speak to one of the cabos,' he hastily added.

'The superior chief wishes to speak to you.'

'Alvarez?'

'Señor.'

'I have received no report from you.'

'But . . . I gave it to you this morning.'

'I am referring to a report on today's work. Or am I being unduly optimistic to assume there has been any?'

'I have hardly had time to have lunch.'

'Your measure of work achieved is judged by how long you have had in which to eat? Were you able to leave the dining table long enough to question Heron?'

'I did so at considerable length.'

'Does he admit owning a gun?'

'Says he's never had one and Teresa is making up the story of seeing an automatic in the drawer.'

'Can he explain why she should do that?'

'Only that it is to harm him.'

'Why should she wish to?'

'He did not say.'

'And you did not attempt to make him clarify what he'd said?'

'I don't think he really knew what he was saying. He was in a very emotional state. He also denied ever having possessed ammunition.'

'If he denies owning a gun, is he likely to admit he has some ammunition?'

'Of course not.'

'Then his denial was logical; your question to him, illogical.'

'Two shots were fired.'

'I am aware of that fact.'

'So two cases were ejected.'

'You find that surprising?'

'Two cases were in a flowerbed outside the front door.'

'I am also aware of that fact.'

'I have sent them to Forensics, together with a metal case for a pack of cigarettes.'

'You included the cigarettes?'

'No.'

'Nor a box of matches to make certain they lacked for nothing?'

'I don't think you understand, señor.'

'That is percipient of you.'

'Forensics needed Heron's fingerprints to check whether they were on the cartridge cases, so I asked him if he could identify the cigarette case and gave it to him to hold.'

There was a brief silence.

'You are conversant with the works of Carolina Ramos?' Salas asked.

'I am afraid not.'

'She is held to be intelligent, even though a woman. In one of her books, she wrote, "It is more likely to be true if it appears impossible."'

Another silence.

'You have nothing to say?' Salas asked sharply.

'It seems rather illogical, señor.'

'Then consider the fact that you appear to have acted with intelligence. Can you yet say whether a shot fired in Ca'n Ajo will be heard outside Cana Llagena and its direction judged with some accuracy?'

'I have arranged the tests. And I have spoken to Doctor Noguero about the slight inconsistency of the time of the shot and his judgment as to the time of death. He is slightly surprised, but content to accept that he was a little wrong with his estimate. I have also learned the name and address of the man who was suspected of carrying out the burglary at Ca'n Ajo.'

'Is his evidence relevant to the present case?'

'I haven't yet had a chance to question him.'

'What has the insurance company said?'

'As I may have mentioned, señor, I have been pursuing so many leads that I cannot find the time to do everything.'

'Pay less regard to eating and you will succeed. Report to me as soon as you learn any results.'

As ever, Salas did not bother to say goodbye. Alvarez replaced the receiver.

'You are again looking very tired, Enrique,' Dolores said.

'I feel totally exhausted.' Alvarez sat at the dining room table.

'Is the work so very hard?'

'It's not that so much as Salas.'

'What has that beastly man been doing now?'

'Demanding I do ten things at once.'

'He is a slave driver. His forbears must have been Barbary pirates.'

'Why them?' Jaime asked.

'You do not know how they treated those they had captured? They shackled them to the thwarts of their galleys and made them row to the beat of a drum, lashed them with horrible whips if they lost the timing or didn't look to be using all their energy.'

'And Salas has been whipping Enrique? S and M in the Cuerpo!'

'You can believe that is humorous?' Dolores asked in tones of absolute zero. 'As my mother used to say, every time a husband tells a joke, his wife has reason to bow her head in shame.' She turned to Alvarez. 'I have prepared *Bacalao a la Extremeña*. Eat well and you will not feel so tired. And since it will be a little time more before I serve, have a drink.'

'He's not the only one feeling tired,' Jaime said.

'His tiredness comes from work.' She went into the kitchen.

Jaime watched Alvarez fill his glass, looked round to make certain his wife was not standing behind the bead curtain before he reached for the bottle.

Fifteen

Mestara was a large village in the Pla plain – a flat region of what was now very fertile land. Over 200 years before, it had largely been swampy and a visiting Frenchman had suggested 1,000 hectares be reclaimed to grow rice and vegetables. Being a foreigner, the locals marked him as a fool and his proposals plain madness. Nevertheless, when malaria had been controlled and the local contempt for foreigners had abated, the scheme was finally undertaken and thanks to underground springs the land proved so fertile that potatoes could be cropped three times a year and rice, of high quality, grew so well that Mestara became known as the rice village.

Being inland, it was largely untroubled by tourists, though some visited it on market day because the variety of vegetables was considerable, in season the strawberries were delicious, and prices were lower than in markets by the coast. The streets were narrow, the houses largely stone built and terraced, and there were still many corner shops despite the supermarket on the outskirts. In January, there were the *foguerons* – bonfires in the streets around which danced masked men and in which the figures of devils were burned to prove the victory of good over evil. The next morning, *espinagadas* – pies with vegetables and freshwater eels – were cooked for visiting friends to enjoy. The centuries retreated.

Alvarez swore. He thought he knew the town well, but it had taken him ten minutes to find Carrer Aragon amongst the maze of streets and there was nowhere along it to park. Enough was enough. There was a space in front of a house, on the wall of which was a plaque, issued by the town hall, denying the right of anyone to park there other than the owner of the house. He drew into it.

The walk, which proved to be even longer than he had feared, did not improve his well-being. There was no wind and the narrow streets captured the heat, causing him to sweat profusely, breathe rapidly, and wonder if the doctor might not be absurd to say he needed to give up smoking and to drink far less.

He opened the door of number fifteen and stepped into the *entrada*. There could hardly have been a greater difference than with his own home. The seating of the single chair needed repairing, the walls were shadowed with dust, there was no embroidered linen cloth on the table and no flowers. He called out.

A woman came through the open inner doorway, stared antagonistically at him. 'Yes?'

The people of Llueso had always considered those from Mestara to lack manners and grace. Her hair looked as though it had not recently been combed or brushed, she wore no make-up, her clothes were suited only for working in the field; she had greeted him with suspicion, not the pleasantness which was to be expected. 'You are Domingo Cortes's wife?'

She said nothing.

'I wish to speak to him.'

'He's asleep.'

'Wake him up.'

'Who are you, coming in here and giving orders? From Llueso, from the sound of you.' Her tone added that that was something of which to be ashamed.

'Inspector Alvarez, Cuerpo General de Policia.'

'Why didn't you say so?' she muttered. 'I'll wake him.' She left.

Alvarez was tired but did not sit; the chair looked incapable of bearing much weight – not that his weight was much. He crossed to the far wall, on which hung a faded photograph in a simple, stained wooden frame. A woman, not young but not yet clearly middle-aged, was wearing traditional working costume – close-fitting black bodice, secured with a pin at the front, lace coif and full skirt. Her long plait hung down under the coif. He thought back to when he had been young and there had still been those who maintained the habit of meeting on a Sunday, dressed in traditional costumes, sometimes adorned with gold buttons and chains and with *mantós* – richly embroidered, hand-made shawls.

There was sound behind him and he turned. Cortes had been described as small-time; noticing the mean features, the thin lips offering an uneasy smile, Alvarez added 'sly, cunning'. 'Domingo Cortes?'

Cortes nodded.

'I've some questions you'll answer.'

He looked down at the ground.

'It's going to take time, so where do we sit?'

Cortes looked briefly at the outside door with vain hope, turned and walked through the inner doorway.

Alvarez was surprised to enter a room that was clean and well furnished; the flat-screen TV was large and by its side was a music centre. For some, crime did occasionally pay. He was not going to be asked to sit, so he sat. The chair was comfortable and probably expensive.

He studied Cortes.

'What . . . what is it?' Cortes finally asked, his thin, reedy voice pitched high.

'I want to hear about your two visits to Ca'n Ajo.'

'Where?'

'Hard of hearing?'

'Don't know the place.'

'Señora Heron was shot there a week ago.'

'Why come here about that?'

'Because you visited the house a few months back.'

'Never been near it.'

'As usual, helped yourself to equipment which could be sold easily and anonymously.'

'I tell you, I was never there.'

'The local policia think differently.'

'Wouldn't listen to what I said. I told 'em to prove it was me. They couldn't.'

'Because you'd moved the loot too quickly?'

'They'd nothing on me so there wasn't nothing they could do. Only they still name me when there ain't no reason.'

'It's a rough life in your chosen profession. They told me you had a smart way of opening shutters.'

'Don't know what that means.'

'You've designed a piece of equipment which will open closed shutters from the outside. Very efficient, but leaves identifiable marks in the woodwork. Kind of a signature, I suppose one could say.'

'Have they ever found whatever it is I'm supposed to have made?'

'You know the answer to that. If they had, you'd be in jail.'

'It's just them talking big.'

'Suppose I explain that I'm interested because a shutter at Ca'n Ajo now bears your signature?'

'You ain't saying—'

'That you returned the night Señora Heron was murdered? That's what interests me, yes.'

'I couldn't kill anyone.'

'It's not very difficult if one has a gun.'

'You think I'd kill a woman?'

'If you had to, to save your own skin.'

'I wasn't near the place,' Cortes said desperately.

'Then where were you?'

'When? You've got me all confused.'

'We're talking about midnight, a week ago today.'

'I was here.'

'Prove it.'

'She'll tell you.'

'Her evidence won't weigh a gram.'

'We was together all night.'

'Neighbours will tell me they saw you go out in your car that night. You know the routine as well as I do.'

'I swear I wasn't near Ca'n Ajo.'

'You and a companion – an efficient peterman – broke into the house believing, after careful surveillance, that it was empty. Whilst your companion examined the safe, you looked around and found an automatic Colt in a drawer. Guns are worth money so even if the contents of the two safes were a fortune, you weren't throwing away a few extra euros. So you pocketed the gun. You told your companion and he, judging you'd never dare use it, demanded you give it to him for insurance.

'What you had no way of knowing was that Señora Heron was returning from England. So when she suddenly appeared, you panicked, he shot her to escape the chance of identification. But unless you admit that now and identify him, you are going to be held as much a murderer as he. The garrotte may have been abolished, but murder carries a very long prison sentence and you'll be a fool to risk that when, by telling the truth, you can be found guilty only of burglary – that is, if you didn't encourage him to shoot the señora.'

'I wasn't there,' he said frantically.

'You'd rather be tried for murder than tell the truth?'

'Ana, Ana!' he shouted wildly.

She rushed into the room.'

'He says . . . he says I killed her. I never did. I wasn't there. For God's sake, tell him I wasn't!'

She put her arms around him, murmured as if comforting a baby. She stared over his shoulder at Alvarez, her face twisted with hatred. 'What are you saying?'

'That either he or his companion killed Señora Heron; that in my opinion it is far more likely the other man did and therefore it's very much in his interests to say now who his companion was and exactly what happened.'

'I wasn't there,' Cortes moaned.

'Him a murderer?' Her voice grew shriller. 'He couldn't hurt anyone. Can't you see that, or are you blind?'

'Which is why I keep asking him to tell me what happened.'

'Nothing happened,' Cortes shouted. 'I wasn't there.'

'He was here,' she said.

'When are we talking about?' Alvarez asked.

She hesitated only briefly. 'He's been here all week. Didn't feel well.'

'He saw a doctor?'

'He's often like that and nothing does him good, so I don't bother with doctors any more.'

'Did friends visit you who can confirm you were both here on the night of the murder?'

She spoke with fresh desperation. 'He was, like I said.'

'Don't you understand—' He stopped. She did not want to understand and she would lie her way into hell if that would defend Cortes.

He left.

He thought Salas would have left for lunch, but was unlucky.

'Señor, I am back from questioning Cortes. He was certainly involved in the burglary at Ca'n Ajo which took place a few months ago and in which electronic equipment was stolen—'

'Repetition is not the key to comprehensive reporting.'

'I am not quite certain what you mean.'

'Every time you have occasion to speak to me, you repeat much of what you have said before.'

'Yet when I do not explain what I am saying—'

'I am meeting a senior member of the Cuerpo in a short time so if you have anything of consequence to report, report it.'

'I think it likely Cortes was involved in the murder of Señora Heron.'

'So you have already said.'

'He became very uneasy when he realized I was questioning him concerning the murder of the señora. He was suffering panicky guilt.'

'Men of his nature do not suffer guilt.'

'Apprehension, then.'

'Kindly say what you mean.'

'He appealed to his woman to support his alibi.'

'His woman?'

'The woman with whom he lives.'

'You are referring to his wife?'

'I doubt they're married.'

'A couple living together in honesty does not appeal to you?'

'With more and more couples not bothering to get married— But it's not really of any account.'

'Then why raise the matter?'

'You asked me if I was referring to Cortes's wife.'

'Which required a one word answer, not a discursion on the corrupt morals of modern youth. Now, answer the question.'

'She was not wearing a ring on her left hand, but there is the possibility she suffers from rheumatism—'

'What the devil does rheumatism have to do with anything?'

'It can be too painful to wear a ring if the finger is swollen . . . Or perhaps I am thinking of arthritis.'

'It has to be doubted you are thinking. The Tower of Babel was said to have led to the confusion of languages; you are capable of causing confusion in just one. Did this female verify Cortes's alibi?'

'She tried to, but it was clearly false confirmation.'

'Your proof?'

'Her manner. She claimed he had been ill, but had not seen a doctor since there was no point in consulting one when they were unable to cure him. She clearly has great affection for him, therefore if he were genuinely ill, she would get him to a doctor immediately.'

'I asked for proof, not conjecture.'

'It could be possible to find the evidence that Cortes was not at home that night.'

'You have started questioning neighbours?'

'I thought the first thing to do was to tell you that I am reasonably certain he was present in Ca'n Ajo when Señora Heron was killed.'

'And Heron?'

'How do you mean?'

'He returned home and soon after a shot was heard. Since he has made no mention of armed intruders, does that not make nonsense of what you've just been saying?'

'I am not certain why it should.'

'I would not expect you to understand too quickly.'

'But you told me—'

'What?'

'Nothing, señor.'

'More repetition. Continue.'

'Riba is dubious he would have heard a shot fired in Ca'n Ajo when he was on the road side of Cana Llagena.'

'Does your test confirm that doubt?'

'We have not yet been able to conduct the test.'

'Because you have not set it up? If my other inspectors worked as diligently and efficiently as you, this island would become a Shangri-La for any mafia.'

'Where?'

'To explain would increase your confusion. You will carry out the test the moment this conversation is over.'

'Then if it proves the first shot would not have been heard by Riba, the problem you raised can be explained. Cortes and his companion were in the house when the señora unexpectedly returned. Finding the door unlocked, she made her way upstairs, no doubt determined to address her husband bitterly—'

'Why?'

'Riba had told her over the mobile that her husband was with Señora Rowley. But instead of meeting him, she was confronted by the two intruders. They had taken no steps to hide their identities, not expecting such a necessity, so she would be able to identify them. Cortes, despite that fact, would have done nothing but run; his companion was of a different character and shouted at Cortes to shoot her. When Cortes did nothing, he grabbed the gun and fired. A poor shot, he did not kill her, although the force with which she collapsed from the wound in her thigh may have seemed to have fatally injured her.

'They fled the house. Cortes would have been horror-struck by what had happened, his companion merely thankful a gun had been handy.

'The señor returned home, found his wife dying, but not quickly enough because she was in excruciating pain. That would have rendered any man emotionally shattered, but his emotions were further tortured by guilt – he had just returned from Señora Rowley. As the señora screamed in agony, he suffered such a mental apocalypse, he knew only that he had to end her agony. He shot her in a mercy killing.'

After a while, Salas said, 'Baron Munchausen would admire your reconstruction.'

'He has information which would corroborate it?'

'It is seldom a person has the ability to expose so clearly his lack of literacy and his love of absurdity in one sentence.' Salas rang off.

Sixteen

'You want to know which way the wind was blowing on the evening of the eighteenth of July?' asked the harbourmaster.

'That's it,' Alvarez replied, as he stared through the nearer window at a very large motor cruiser and half of his mind wondered how many tens of thousands of euros a month she cost to run.

The harbourmaster opened a leather-bound logbook and turned the pages until he found the one he wanted. He ran a forefinger down the entries. 'Light winds from the south-east.'

'South-east?'

'There's a problem?'

'At least a question mark.'

Alvarez stood on the road side of Cana Llagena, aware that Hilary Rowley was staring at him through a window. Was she trying to work out what he was doing? Had Heron phoned her earlier? He raised the mobile to his mouth. 'Fire one in ten seconds, shutters closed.'

'Shall I do it with a countdown from ten?'

He ignored the childish question. The wind was very light, perhaps as it had been on that Thursday night, but it was coming from the north-east and assisting sound to travel rather than hindering it.

He heard nothing.

'Shutters open, fire two.'

Once more, silence. As Riba had judged, on the road side of the house, in calm conditions, a shot would not be heard.

He walked round the house and faced the belt of trees. 'With shutters closed, fire three.'

A dog began to bark, and two more joined in. He heard no shot. He had not considered dogs. Since they barked intermittently throughout day and night, Salas would name such omission gross incompetence. 'Wait until there's no barking, then fire again.'

He heard no shot. 'Fire three, shutters open.'

'It's four. Need help with counting?'

'Fire with the muzzle against your head.'

Minutes passed before there was a temporary lull in the barking. The sound of the shot was audible, but only just. Would one identify it unless one knew a pistol was being fired?

Riba could not have been expecting to hear a shot. The wind had been hindering sounds travelling to him. Dogs were once more barking, so any lull would have been brief . . . Did the copy of the letter to Riba in Señora Heron's safe hold even more importance than he had previously assigned it? Belinda Heron had written to Riba in insulting terms and must have given great offence. His was the only evidence that—

'What are we waiting for? To try out the artillery?'

'That's tomorrow. Thanks for your help.'

He switched off his mobile, returned it to his pocket. There was no known reason to doubt Riba's evidence that Heron had left Cana Llangera at 2317, but what if his evidence that he had heard a shot at 0010 was false? Then Heron's evidence became acceptable. He had arrived home, found the door unlocked, searched for an intruder, found his wife murdered . . . Allow a generous ten-minute walk from house to house, a minute or two outside the unlocked door – he might well have hesitated – there was a gap of over an hour before he reported her death. Why? Had he been temporarily shocked into an inability to do anything? That could have happened, since the mind had a greater control over the body than was sometimes accepted. Yet Heron had poured himself a whisky and drunk it, as witness the empty glass in his wife's bedroom. In times of great stress, a man could easily turn to drink. And the champagne? Merely evidence that she drank more than she would have admitted?

* * *

'You're naming Riba a second suspect simply because she had annoyed him?' Salas asked, as dismissively as if considering little green men from Mars.

'Señor, perhaps you do not appreciate the Mallorquin character—'

'Not something to appreciate.'

'To accuse a man of theft or swindling—'

'There is no need to repeat what you have said before, frequently and at great length. Have you questioned Riba again?'

'I intend to do so as soon as possible.'

'You will do so before then, even if there is small probability that to do so will in any way further the progression of the case.'

'Señor?'

'Well?'

'It's not very long ago that you rebuked me for expecting failure.'

'Because you lack the ability to think progressively or in depth.' Salas rang off.

Ferrer was seated on a patio chair by the swimming pool, allowing time to flow gently past.

'All the weeds under control?' Alvarez asked.

'A chap needs a break now and then to recover.'

'That's true.'

'What's brought you back?'

'I need to have a chat with you.' Alvarez crossed to the pool house and brought out another chair, which he put down near Ferrer.

The water had not a ripple across it; its cool calmness projected a sense of smooth peace and Alvarez might have fallen asleep had not Ferrer said, 'So what's the chat about?'

'This and that.'

'Asking for more garlic, are you?'

'That wasn't the intention, but now you've mentioned the possibility, I'll not refuse the offer.'

'There ain't no offer.'

'Dolores will be very disappointed. Since she used a little

of the little you gave me, she's been smiling all day. And
the kids have been eating like never before and telling her
how wonderful her cooking has become. Makes a mother
proud to be praised by her children . . . What has your wife
thought about your problems over the gambling?'

Ferrer didn't answer.

'Maybe, like a wise man, you don't bother her with the
complications of your life?'

'What's it to you?'

He watched a hummingbird hawkmoth investigate one
of the red and yellow flowers of a nearby lantana. 'It must
have infuriated you.'

'What must?'

'The señora accusing you of stealing the garlic.'

'Just made me laugh.'

'Because you thought how you'd get your own back?'

'Are you on about that again?'

'I'm thinking how I'd feel in similar circumstances. I'd
be so furious, I'd tell her what a bitch she was and what a
bitch everyone else thinks her. Being the woman she was,
she'd start abusing me, likely saying all my ancestors lived
in caves and were thieves. On this island, an insult to an
ancestor is rightly more insulting than an insult to oneself;
I can answer back, they can't. So her words would enrage
me until I might well threaten her physically if she didn't
shut up. That would really make her mad – a peasant laying
a hand on her! It would also frighten her so she'd seek something with which to defend herself and produce her husband's
automatic. Obviously, she would have no idea how to handle
a gun, so I would be afraid she'd shoot me unintentionally
and I'd try to take it from her with fatal results.'

'You talk more balls than a politician.'

'Impossible. In any case, I'm merely suggesting how I'd
feel.'

'You think me soft? You're accusing me of shooting her,
only you ain't got the guts to say so outright.'

'I'll try to summon up the necessary courage. Did you
shoot Señora Heron?'

'I've said before.'

'I don't remember, so say again.'

'Of course I bloody didn't. Kill her just because she was a bitch and called me a thief?'

'She was threatening to take all the garlic from you, which would leave you at the mercy of the enforcers. So you would be saving your own skin. Where were you a week ago yesterday, from ten at night onwards?'

'Where d'you think I was?'

'Waiting outside this house until certain it was clear to go in and tell her what you thought of her.'

'When she wasn't here? And if I wanted to do that, I'd do it in working time, not when I ain't paid to be here.'

There might be some logic in that, Alvarez accepted. 'You were at home?'

'Of course I was.'

'Your wife will corroborate you?'

'Yes.'

'How d'you know until you ask her?'

'Because I was at home, that's bloody why!'

Alvarez used a handkerchief to wipe the sweat from his forehead, face and neck.

'If you ain't anything more to say, I'm moving.'

'By the way, I don't like interrupting a man when he's working, so it'll be best if when I ask your wife to check your alibi, which of course she will, I have another word about the señora's behaviour.'

'What's stopping you asking now?'

'I don't have the questions sorted out.'

'And you don't remember me telling you that the wife didn't know about me gambling?'

'I had forgotten.'

'And you're sorry, but even though now you've remembered, you'll still have to come and ask in front of her?'

'Maybe.'

'In your own quiet way, you're as big a bastard as anyone.'

Seventeen

The first person at the Bourne Insurance Company to whom Alvarez spoke seemed uncertain about how to deal with the request, finally suggested he had a word with Mrs Easton. Alvarez had never really reconciled himself to discussing business with a woman, feeling that was unnatural; however, he had learned to conceal the fact.

'Good morning,' Mrs Easton said briskly. 'I understand I am speaking to Inspector Alvarez of the Spanish police?'

'That is correct, señora.'

'How can I help you?'

Her clipped, authoritative voice pictured in his mind severe hairstyle, ice cold eyes, long nose, thin lips and aggressive chin. 'I should like to ask for the details of a life insurance policy which has been taken out with your company.'

'We can give no such information, Inspector, without an official application made by a senior member of the police.'

'All I need to know is if the policy has been cancelled.'

'I am not certain we can even tell you that without an official request.'

It gave her a sense of power to refuse. Pity the man who worked under her authority.

'It is very important.'

'I am certain it is or you would not have bothered to phone.'

Then why didn't she do what any intelligent Mallorquin would and tell him what he wanted to know in a sideways manner that broke no rules? 'I am investigating a murder.'

'I'm sorry to hear that.'

Only in public. She would be indifferent to the tragedies of others.

'Lives may indirectly depend on our quickly catching the perpetrator.'

'Perhaps if you explain how the information would be of assistance to your inquiries, I could seek immediate authority to reveal what you need to know?'

He would have liked to tell her that details of the case could only be given on written authority from high, but he sensed that she lacked any sense of humour.

'We are trying to discover if any important papers are missing from a safe in the victim's home. There is a list of assets which include a life insurance policy and a reference number is given, but there is nothing more to confirm the entry. We wonder if the policy has been cancelled, but not noted as such, and that is why there is no confirmation?' A little white lie never hurt anyone, he told himself.

'If you will give me the name and the policy number, I will check as quickly as I can.'

He did as she asked.

'One moment, please.'

As he waited, he wondered what Dolores would be cooking for lunch. It was some time since she had served paella – not the paella tourists knew, but *a la Valenciana*, containing chicken, pork, hake, eel, crayfish, prawns, mussels, octopus, beans, peas, artichoke hearts, onions, pimientos, saffron, olive oil . . .

'Sorry to keep you waiting.'

'It has been no time.'

'I am allowed to tell you that the policy has not been cancelled, but nothing more.'

Had he asked for anything more? 'Thank you.'

Dolores might not have had the time to make the paella since it should never be cooked in a hurry. Perhaps *pollo asado a la llodra*? Plenty of white wine and many rashers of bacon on a full-breasted chicken which was cooked in lard . . .

'Inspector, you said there has been a murder. May I ask, was Mrs Heron the victim?'

'I am afraid so.'

'Oh, dear!'

A conventional response. He thanked her for her help,

said goodbye, replaced the receiver. He had a drink before he phoned Salas.

'Señor, I have just spoken to Señora Easton—'

'Am I to be allowed the privilege of knowing who she is?'

'I am afraid I don't know her position in the firm—'

'There are those who say there are parallel universes. If true, it seems I live in one and you in another. I did not ask what was her position in the firm for which she works.'

'But—'

'Well?'

'She's with the Bourne Insurance Company in London and has just told me that Señora Heron's life insurance has not been cancelled.'

'Are you capable of appreciating what that means?'

'It does suggest—' Alvarez stopped.

'Who benefits from the valid policy?'

'Señor Heron.'

'Who knew he would inherit nothing else from his wife, almost certainly because she had learned of his affair. The house and her jewellery went to others and so, on her death, all he could hope to inherit was—'

'Señor?'

'Do I have to have you gagged before you cease to interrupt me?'

'To date, we do not know to what extent he knew about her financial affairs.'

'Was he not her husband?'

'The will was in her safe.'

'Why should that prevent his reading it?'

'After the burglary and when the assessor wanted her to check her valuables, it seems she refused to allow her husband to open the safe and insisted on doing so herself. That suggests she might not have allowed him any knowledge of her financial affairs.'

'You never told me about that. In any case, it would be quite unnatural for a husband not to know about all his wife's business.'

'I don't think it's so unusual in England.'

'The more one learns about them, the more explainable it is that they had a woman prime minister.'

'And a queen as tough as any man. Look how Queen Elizabeth dealt with our Armada—'

'She did not "deal with it", as you so ignorantly and inelegantly suggest. As a Spaniard, even if a Mallorquin, you should know it was solely the treacherous weather around that treacherous island which caused our ships to retreat. Why are you wasting my time ignorantly discussing the Armada?'

'You referred to Señora Thatcher—'

'I did not mention her name. Have you anything of consequence to report?'

'There has to be the possibility that Señor Heron knew the details of his wife's will.'

'Are you able to reach any conclusion without immediately denying its possibility?'

'The señora's last will was dated at about the time she employed Riba, the private detective—'

'Dammit, must you repeat everything fifteen times?'

'So she knew about, or strongly suspected, her husband's affair with Señora Rowley and decided to disinherit him. She was a spiteful woman, so it is reasonable to suppose she told him what she was doing to enjoy the pleasure of his bitter despair.'

'Whether or not Heron was aware of the contents of her will is, thanks to your confusion, a matter beyond clarification for the moment. However, what is clear is that he knew about the life insurance and since it had not been specifically identified in the will it would be included in the remainder of the estate, which had been left to him. Without a house or an income of any weight, he would be very hard up without the sum guaranteed by that insurance.

'Not long before her death, probably very few days, Señora Heron realized that unless her will was changed, her husband would inherit a quarter of a million pounds from the insurance. That is why she drafted a new will. She wrote "Cancelled" on the policy, believing that when she did legally cancel it, she would be denying him any benefit from it—'

'Why cancel and presumably lose the money she had paid rather than leaving the benefit to another named person?'

'Did I not order you to cease interrupting me?'

'Yes, señor. Only it does seem an important question to try to answer because—'

'Heron learned she intended to cancel the policy and so had to act very quickly. He shot her before she could effect the cancellation and then ineffectually tried to make out she had been killed by some intruder, no doubt remembering the earlier burglary.'

'But the insurance money sounds a lot until it is translated into income when invested. Such income would have been very considerably less than his wife received, so it seems odd he should kill her. After all, she might be a very difficult woman, but she maintained a style of living he enjoyed while he was getting his bit on the side—'

'What bit?'

'An expression.'

'Meaning what?'

'That he was enjoying the favours of Señora Rowley.'

'It is extraordinary that you seem unable to think of anything other than sex.'

'It is very important.'

'To those with no self-control or self-respect.'

'Important to this case. The señor was married to a shrew of a woman, but she was rich. It was sex which drew him to Señora Rowley.'

'You find it impossible to accept that initially it was simply a meeting of common interests?'

'I suppose one could hold that that is what I'm saying.'

'You deliberately misunderstand me?'

'Of course not, señor.'

'You are unaware that there are those for whom sex is of no great importance?'

There were those who thought the earth was flat.

'Heron,' Salas continued, 'realized that if he did not act quickly, he would face the prospect of enduring a life very far from one of luxury, since the hiring of a private detective by his wife inevitably indicated divorce. Lacking any morality, he murdered his wife before she could legally cancel the life insurance.'

'Why not continue it and leave the proceeds of its maturity to a specific person?'

'You have already posed that question.'

'I don't think you have answered it.'

'A superior chief does not hold his position of authority in order to answer his juniors. You will question Heron regarding the policy, you will gain evidence that he knew his wife intended to cancel it in order to prevent his benefiting, and you will arrest him.'

'But I still have to speak to Riba.'

'About what?'

'I can't be certain until I question him. You mustn't forget—'

'I do not forget.'

'You will remember Señora Heron had accused him of falsifying the hours he said he worked on her behalf—'

'I have the impression you are yet again going to suggest the insult to Riba's pride raises a motive for the murder.'

'If the señora had challenged his honesty, he might have lost the licence to act as a private detective. That must provide a strong motive.'

There was a pause before Salas said. 'You will question him again to discover if there is any evidence which inculpates him.'

'If there is, his evidence concerning the señor's leaving Cana Llangena at 2317 is probably correct, but hearing a shot at 0010 is not. Señor Heron's innocence is restored and his evidence becomes valid . . . That will still leave one problem.'

'You are about to declare that what you have just suggested is possible, is impossible?'

'Señora Rowley agreed that Señor Heron left her house at around 2315 because he was due to collect his wife from the airport. The walk should not have taken fifteen minutes, more likely around ten, so he arrived home before, or by, 2330. The shot was heard at 0010 and he did not report his wife's death until 0045. Why was there this gap?'

'You have an answer which you can immediately contradict?'

'Shock. Finding his wife dead occasioned the most severe shock which disorientated his brain—'

'You are a neurologist?'

'I think it reasonable to suppose it took time for him to recover sufficiently to realize what needed to be done.'

'We will bring all these surmises to an end. You will question Riba. Assuming you learn nothing of significance from him, you will question Heron and, as I said before, arrest him.'

Alvarez replaced the receiver. There probably was enough circumstantial evidence to warrant the arrest of Heron, but . . . He lit a cigarette. Why had Belinda acted so out of character as to give the staff time off that day? Why had she written 'Cancelled' on the insurance policy when it had not been? Had she taken steps to cancel it which had not been implemented? Had she written to the company – there was no record of her having done so amongst her papers – but not had the chance to send the letter before her death? Why, as he had repeatedly queried with Salas, had she not named someone to enjoy the proceeds?

Questions which disappeared if one accepted Heron had killed her in order to enjoy happiness and such income as her death would provide, rather than continue to suffer unhappiness and luxury. Yet he simply could not accept that.

Alvarez settled at the dining room table and poured a thirsty man's measure of brandy into which he dropped four ice cubes.

'Amando was here during the morning,' Jaime said. 'Guess why he came?'

'To borrow something long-term.'

'To bring us half a sucking pig.'

'At this time of the year? And what does he want in return?' To give was to expect to receive.

'Can't say, being at work when he was here.'

'Is it fresh?'

'She didn't say it wasn't.'

'But he might have found it dead and won't risk eating it himself.'

Dolores came through the bead curtain, stopped, folded her arms across her ample bosom. 'So very typical! Neither my husband nor my cousin can understand there are some people in this world who are thoughtful, kind and generous.'

If, Alvarez thought, she really believed Amando was any of those things . . .

'The selfish man can see only selfishness. Amando came here because neither he nor María has seen us for many weeks and they wanted to know if we were all well.'

'He could have phoned to find out,' Jaime observed.

'Spoken by a man who seldom brings pleasure to others because he thinks only of himself.'

'That's not right.'

'You are correct. I should have said "never".'

'It's no time since I drove you into Palma simply because you wanted to go there.'

'Yet many, many days after I first asked because the matter was urgent; and it was only after you had arranged to meet Pedro in the Plaza Major.'

'What makes you believe that stupidity?'

'Pedro phoned before we left to make certain you had remembered the meeting.'

'You . . . you never told me.'

'There was no need. I was able to assure him you would be there since you had unwillingly suggested I might also like to go to Palma.'

'The only reason I arranged to meet Pedro was because I knew I was going to take you.'

'Then he was mistaken when he said you'd made the arrangement with him the previous week, several days before you asked me?'

'He's got it wrong.'

'You should remember that nothing breeds faster than a lie.' She returned to the kitchen.

Eighteen

Alvarez had not expected Riba to be round, cheerful and more like a favourite uncle than someone who grubbed into other people's lives. He had been equally surprised, to judge from the office's prime location in Inca, the quality of the furnishings, and the smart, young, attractive secretary, how profitable the occupation of private detective must be.

Riba had plump fingers, but his handshake was firm. 'Have a seat, Inspector.'

Alvarez sat. The comfort of the chair spelled quality and cost.

'Before we start, would you like some coffee?'

'Thank you.'

Riba used the small intercom on his desk to ask Beatriz to make coffee for them. He settled back in his chair. 'Since you're from Llueso and Señora Heron was a client of mine, I imagine this visit is connected with her death?'

'Yes.'

'There is some way in which I may be able to help the investigation?'

'There could be.'

Riba smiled a broad, chubby smile. 'Perhaps I should tell you that I was born and lived in Valencia until eight years ago.'

Something Alvarez had already discerned. Riba spoke Mallorquin with an accent and occasional unusual choice of word or grammatic structure.

'While living there, I joined the Cuerpo, so I know all too well how a true detective regards a private one. Like a cow looking at what it leaves behind.'

'Once an inspector, always an inspector,' Alvarez said, accepting the need to refrain from any appearance of superiority.

Riba picked up a silver paper knife and fingered the hilt. 'I became fed up with dealing with people who made crime more profitable than was my job and so I followed the advice of a retired brigada who told me that if I wanted a good life, I should quit the Cuerpo and work for rich old men who married pretty young women and wondered why they went to the gym so often and for rich old women who were worried because their young husbands were suddenly kind and thoughtful. The brigada was correct. My work may be very limited in variety, but I run a new BMW instead of a second-hand Seat.'

'I must consider the possibility.'

'Not before I retire, please, because there are only enough octogenarians at this end of the island to offer work for one.'

Alvarez dutifully smiled. 'Following Señora Heron's murder, we naturally searched the house very thoroughly. In her safe was the copy of a letter addressed to you.'

'Probably one of many, since I had endless letters from her and even more phone calls, all complaining. A very difficult woman.'

'Her staff would agree.'

'And her husband?'

Alvarez did not answer.

'If what I've read in the paper is correct, he must be the prime suspect?'

'We don't have one as yet.'

'In other words, no comment. . . . The copy of the letter is of some particular interest?'

'In it, she complained you were charging her for many more hours of work than you were carrying out.'

'One of her favourite moans. Another was that the evidence I was collecting wasn't strong enough. I think she wanted me to hide in a bedroom cupboard. It is a fact that a spouse wanting a divorce demands all the sordid details. A touch of masochism, perhaps.'

'She threatened you.'

'With what, this time? Only paying half the bill?'

'With reporting you for swindling her.'

'Oh! One of her more vicious efforts!'

'To whom could she complain?'

'You haven't checked?'

'More important things to do.'

'But now you can afford to waste a little time on the less important ones?'

Alvarez drank the last of the coffee, replaced the cup on the saucer. Riba had spoken lightly, but with an undercurrent of . . . of what? Fear, concern, resentment, anger?

'To whom, could she complain?' he asked a second time.

'The administrative committee. There are not many of us on the island, although resident expatriates have helped to expand our numbers, but we can only work with a licence from the state and that calls for a committee of elected members. Any complaint is sent to the secretary of the committee, who places it before them, and they decide whether it is spurious or serious. In the latter instance, the person is asked for his comments and the papers are sent to the ministry where it is decided whether to withdraw the offender's licence.'

'That is the only penalty?'

'The only one that hurts. Formal reprimands merely irritate.'

'Had Señora Heron made a formal complaint against you?'

'A barbed question!' Riba smiled broadly and his full cheeks formed folds.

'Yet one that has to be asked and answered.'

'As I imagined, this is not the casual chat you've tried to make out. You are wondering if her letter scared me sufficiently to make me try to change her mind.'

'Did you?'

'I phoned and explained that to be certain beyond any reasonable doubt her husband was conducting an affair took many hours of surveillance; that I always noted times down to the last minute; that I kept a log with all the times and she could read through this if she wished, add up the hours and minutes, and find they were exactly as put down on the account I sent her.'

'If they matched, she wouldn't have doubted the veracity of your log?'

'Probably. Like as not, she would have called it a forgery. She never controlled her tongue or her pen.'

'How did she react to your explanations?'

'Rude disbelief.'

'Leaving you fearing she would forward her complaint?'

'That was a probability.'

'So you were worried?'

Riba stood, opened a silver cigarette case. 'Do you smoke?'

'Thank you.'

Riba drew in smoke, expelled it in a series of smoke rings. 'I mentioned earlier I was in the Cuerpo for some years. That taught me to be suspicious of everyone; a suspicion exacerbated if I met a pleasant reception when I would have expected a hostile one. So while you have been pleasantly curious, I suspect you believe I might in some way be involved in the murder of Señora Heron.'

He waited for a comment. There was none. 'In almost all cases, murder needs a motive. What motive could I have for murdering the señora? My dislike for a rude virago? If one murdered all such women, undertakers would become rich. You have seen a copy of the letter she sent to me and now you know what would be the consequences to me if it was accepted as correct. To lose my licence would be to lose my job and life would no longer be as easy as it is at the moment. So, did I kill her in order to prevent her mailing her complaint or to prevent her substantiating it if she did?'

'What's the answer?'

'You think me capable of murder?'

'In the right circumstances, few are incapable of it.'

'You do not accept that I have the proof I was right and she was wrong and therefore her threats could not harm me?'

'You have admitted that she would have alleged your log was a forgery. The fact remains that, however genuine, it was kept by you without any corroborative evidence to prove you were being honest in what you wrote.'

'My assurance to you that not a word or a figure is a lie is insufficient?'

'Do I need to answer?'

'So I murdered in order to save my own skin?'

'It is a possibility I have to consider.'

'And having considered?'

'I haven't.'

'What now?'

'I have two more questions before I return to Llueso.'

'They are?'

'You told me that after seeing Señor Heron leave Señora Rowley's house, you heard a shot. I have had experimental shots fired to judge how clearly they would be heard.'

'And?'

'In best conditions, the shot was indistinct and could easily have been mistaken unless one knew a gun might be fired.'

'As I have said before, I have no doubts. My hearing has more than once been described as acute.'

'Which way was the wind blowing?'

'I have no idea.'

'That night, it was from Cana Llagena towards Ca'n Ajo.'

'So?'

'Sound that Thursday would not have travelled as clearly as on the day of the test when the wind was blowing in the opposite direction.'

'The inference is obvious, so I need to ask who was in the vicinity of the two houses to judge the direction of the wind?'

'The information came from the harbourmaster.'

'And therefore relates to wind over the bay.'

'There will be little or no difference in direction.'

'I am no expert in – aerology? – but I tend to think that if one is consulted, he will make the point that the mountains ringing the bay may create a different wind pattern from that found six or seven kilometres inland.'

'When did you return home that night?'

'Some time after twelve.'

'Your wife can confirm that?'

'She departed a couple of years ago with a young Italian of smarmy manners.'

'I'm sorry to hear that,' Alvarez said formally.

'Every mountain has its sunny side. I've since met a charming lady.'

'She was with you that night?'

'No. Her husband, a commercial pilot, was not flying.'

'Then you can't offer any corroboration?'

'I could, but I prefer to tell the truth.'

Moments later, Alvarez settled in his car, lowered the window and switched on the fan. Riba distrusted a friendly attitude when an unfriendly one was to be expected; he distrusted a cheerful attitude when fear and antagonism were to be expected.

Nineteen

The telephone rang, threatening Alvarez's homegoing. He waited for several rings, hoping the automatic cut-out would operate and the caller assume he was out, hard at work, but he was unlucky. It did stop ringing, but very quickly began again. He lifted the receiver.

'Inspector Alvarez?'

'Speaking.' Would Dolores be serving an early meal? If so, would she keep him his portion?

'Forensics. You asked for a comparison of prints with those on a metal cigarette case and two cartridge cases, if these bore any. They did and we confirm they match.'

He thanked the other, rang off. He stared at the far wall and in his mind saw Heron coming downstairs, gun in one hand, ejected cases in the other, mind in chaos, opening the front door, stepping outside and throwing the cases away in an impotent gesture of shocked rejection of what he had done, continuing on to the well and dropping the gun into that . . .

There was motive enough. Relations between him and his wife had reached a new low since she had learned he was having an affair. Hiring Riba had signalled divorce and subsequent hardship for him. She had initially forgotten that unless she specifically named the person to whom the proceeds of the life insurance were to be paid, her husband would inherit them under the remainder clause in her will; she had decided to amend that and cancel the policy. Why? Heron had understood that if she died before the cancellation of the policy was completed and her new will became legal, he would inherit the quarter of a million pounds. No fortune, but enough to add comfort to a life with Hilary . . .

Heron would do whatever he could to ensure Hilary was happy. Yet killing his wife was out of character and must surely appal Hilary and end their relationship. But where was the evidence to prove Ferrer, Cortes, or Riba had murdered her, not Heron?

Dolores looked across the dining room table. 'You are again not eating with enthusiasm.'

Alvarez said hastily, and truthfully, 'It's delicious.'

'Then why are you so slow?'

'It's only thinking about work.'

'Has that obnoxious man been worrying you again?'

'He just will not understand how a man's character can be a key to what he will not do.'

'In my experience, there is little a man will not do.'

'You think Jaime could murder you?'

'Sweet Mary! What a thing to ask.'

Jaime said angrily, 'You drink with me, then say I would kill my wife.'

'I suggested no such thing.'

'You wanted to know if I'd kill her.'

'I asked in order to express the impossibility of your doing so.'

'You suggest I would because I wouldn't. You're not just crazy, you're looped.'

'Dolores said there was little a man will not do. I asked if she thought you could kill her. It was a negative question.'

'What's that?'

'One which implies the opposite of what it asks.'

'You've been boozing all day, haven't you?'

'I'll start again. In my opinion, what a man will or will not do can be judged by his character. Dolores suggested there was little a man would not do. I disagree, so I asked her if you would kill her. An impossibility.'

'Then why didn't you say that instead of all the balls about talking one thing and meaning another?'

Alvarez resumed eating.

*   *   *

The next morning he dialled Palma.

'Yes?' said the plum-voiced secretary.

'Is the superior chief in the office today?'

'He is at work every Saturday morning and frequently in the afternoon as well.'

'What about Saturday night?'

'What is your name?' She might have been questioning a man arrested for some abominable crime.

'Inspector Alvarez, speaking from the comarque of Tramuntana.'

'Did the superior chief's directive ask that the name of the comarque be given?'

'No.'

'Did it ask for the name of the commune?'

'No.'

'Then there is no reason to give either. Wait.'

'Yes?' said Salas.

'I have carried out an interview—'

'You do not wish me to know to whom I am speaking?'

'Inspector Alvarez, señor. I didn't say so because recently, when I explained who I was—'

'No explanation could suffice. What is it?'

'I have questioned Riba and am not entirely satisfied with his answers.'

'You will write a comprehensive report on the interrogation and the reasons for your reservations and send it by fax to reach me this afternoon.'

'Señor, I can make a full report now.'

'And when you finish, I will be none the wiser thanks to constant and meaningless interruptions and diversions.'

'I do think you should know now that Forensics have made their report.'

'When did they do so?'

'Yesterday evening.'

'It has taken until now for you to bother to inform me?'

'It was late in the evening, señor.'

'What is your definition of "late"?'

'Well after eight,' he answered, adding a reasonable amount of time.

'I was in my office until nine thirty.'

More fool him. Small wonder rumour suggested that when he joined his wife in bed, he froze.

'In future, you will not judge the working hours of others by your own. What has Forensics reported?'

'The prints on the cartridge cases found in the flowerbed bear Señor Heron's prints.'

'Question him and unless he can offer credible explanations for all the facts which appear to incriminate him, arrest him.'

'I still don't think he killed the señora.'

'Did he deny possession of a gun?'

'Yes.'

'Yet one was seen in his drawer. Did he deny possession of cartridges?'

'But—'

'You fail to appreciate he has lied repeatedly. Why does one lie except to deny guilt? Do I need to keep reminding you of the elementary facts? Heron has betrayed his wife and wishes to live with his mistress; he was seen to leave the woman's home in order to return to his house to collect his wife from the airport; later, a shot was heard—'

'We have conducted firing tests to find out how clearly shots would be heard outside Cana Llagena—'

'Had I not been so rudely interrupted, I would have asked if such tests had finally been carried out.'

'Señor, we have to consider the possibilities that shots would not have been heard or that they might have been heard, but not identified until it was known shots had been fired. At least, not the one which Riba says he heard when at the back of the house. Depending which side one calls the back.'

'A daunting question when posed by a man who turns everything back to front.'

'Riba heard a sound when he was on the side of the house facing Ca'n Ajo. He is certain it was a shot. But when we held the firing tests, shots fired in the bedroom with the windows shut, because of the air conditioning, and shutters both open and shut, were either inaudible or so faint as would likely be ignored unless one knew a gun was likely to be fired. However, Riba claims to have acute hearing. Additionally, on the night of Señora Heron's death, the light wind was from Riba to Ca'n Ajo, whereas on the day of the test, it was in the opposite direction, meaning sound would have carried better.'

'Why have I not learned all this before?'

'I have only recently established the facts.'

'You should have immediately discovered the direction of the wind.'

'There has been so much to do, some things have had to wait.'

'With you in charge of a case, all things wait. You question Riba's evidence?'

'I'm not certain.'

'Does he become a major suspect?'

'He might. He had a motive to kill the señora since she might have ruined his profitable business. If so, he had reason to invent hearing a shot after Señor Heron left Cana Llagena.'

'Following precedent, no doubt you are now about to tell me why there is no reason to suspect Riba.'

'On the contrary. He was paid to uncover proof that Heron was committing adultery. Having done so, why should he have remained outside Cana Llagena? His explanation is that he is very conscientious; yet however conscientious, a man seldom does more than he is paid to do.'

'And as your actions have often testified, often does less than he should.'

'He suggested he wanted to make certain the señor did not return.'

'Why should he imagine that likely?'

'If something had changed and there was reason to allow it, the señor might well have gone back.'

'For what reason?'

'To resume what they had been doing.'

'Your mind is a moral quagmire. Is there any evidence to say Riba knew Heron possessed a gun?'

'No.'

'Are Riba's prints also on the cartridge cases?'

'Only Heron's were on them.'

'Then to regard him as a suspect and Heron uninvolved is as absurd as can be. You will challenge Heron with the known facts and obey my order to consider arresting him if he is unable to show they do not incriminate him.'

Twenty

Teresa opened the front door of Ca'n Ajo and smiled a welcome. 'The señor's gone off with the señora to Palma. That is . . . Señora Rowley is so friendly and he's so fond of her, it seems like she's the señora now. Know what I mean?'

'Of course.'

'Always ready for a quick chat, asks how we are, sympathizes with Eva over her big toe. Couldn't be more different than the other. Even Diego says she's nice.'

'Praise indeed! Have you any idea when the señor will be back?'

'Eva's cooking lunch for them.' She looked at her wristwatch. 'Won't be more than another half hour.'

'Then I'll wait here.' He stepped inside. 'What's Eva cooking?'

'*Perdices en salsa de vino tinto.*'

'It's a long time since I've enjoyed partridge.'

'You like it?'

'Cooked well, it's a dream.'

'They'll be cooked perfectly. Strange, though. Eva said she wanted some chocolate for the sauce. I thought she was joking.'

'Where's the recipe from? Outer Mongolia?'

'She said you'd never tell there was any. That'll be true. I didn't know there were cooks like her before I came here.'

'Sounds as if she's as good as my cousin.'

'From the look of you, that's possible.'

He was uncertain whether that was a compliment to his good health or an unnecessary comment on his waistline.

They heard a phone ring.

'I'd better answer,' Teresa said, 'or Eva will say I'm not doing my job.' She hurried away.

Alvarez moved to his right to look through a window. There was sadness at knowing he would never own so much land. Not that if he did he would waste his time on a garden. Land was meant to be used practically, not for growing inedible plants. Ridge it with a mattock, transfer the seedlings to the ridges so that the roots would be well watered. To eat home-grown peppers, tomatoes, beans, artichokes, lettuces, cucumbers, peas, cauliflowers, cabbages, carrots, onions, melons, pumpkins, to pick a bunch of dessert grapes filled with nectar . . .

'That was the señor.'

He started, turned, faced Teresa.

'Something's happened and they can't get back for lunch and will be eating in Palma. You should have heard Eva when I told her! And she goes for me when I swear a little! I suggested they could have the partridges cold or reheated for supper. Upset her even more. Said the dish had to be eaten the moment it's cooked or it's ruined.'

'All good cooks are temperamental.'

'She's talking about throwing everything into the dustbin.'

'She can't do that!'

'You don't know her when things go wrong.'

'What's stopping you lot doing the eating?'

'We will, but that won't cheer her up . . . Know what, you like partridge so why don't you stay and eat with us?'

'Would Eva mind?'

'Don't see why she should if she's calmed down, but I'd better ask.' She left.

Chocolate with partridge? Still, one could scrape off the sauce when Eva was not looking. He must phone Dolores and provide a plausible excuse – which she would accept – for not returning to lunch.

'Well?' Eva said, as Alvarez ate the last morsel on his plate.

'Superb. Six star.'

'Teresa says your cousin can cook?'

A time for diplomacy. 'She's good, but I have never eaten a dish like this before.' That was true. Dolores was traditional and would never have added chocolate. Yet had he not known this was included, he could not have named it as an ingredient of the sauce, which had been a gastronomic jewel.

Some time later, after a brandy to settle the stomach, he said, 'I suppose I'd better return to work.'

'Like Diego should.'

'I get two hours for lunch,' Ferrer said resentfully.

'And take three.'

Alvarez stood. 'That was a meal never to forget.'

'You'll tell your cousin about it?' Eva asked.

'And when she asks me if you are as good a cook as she, I'll tell her it is impossible to compare caviar with foie gras.'

Eva was slightly underwhelmed with the comparison. It should have been between foie gras and liver pâté.

'I'm sorry you missed lunch,' Dolores said sharply, as Alvarez entered the room.

'No more sorry than I am.'

'I didn't understand why you couldn't return here.'

'The señor was in Palma, but the staff told me they thought he would be back very soon, so I waited. And waited.'

'When did he turn up?'

'Well after three.'

'Then you didn't have much to say to him since it is now only half past three.'

He had spoken without thought.

'Still, I suppose you did have to stay. Have you eaten?'

'They kindly gave me a snack.'

'There is not a cook?'

'Yes. But perhaps she can't cook anything more than snacks.'

'Then you must have a good supper. I shall have to think what to give you.'

'That would be very kind.'

'It is one of my misfortunes that I suffer the desire to be kind to others. Are you going back to work?'

'After a very short siesta.'

He went upstairs to his bedroom, removed his outer clothing, lay on the bed. A delicious lunch to be followed by what would be a delicious supper. There were times when to speak a little less than the truth proved to be kind to both speaker and listener.

Teresa showed Alvarez into the sitting room. Heron, who had been seated on the settee with Hilary, stood, came forward and shook hands. 'I'm sorry we were out this morning.'

'It was of no great matter, señor.'

'Have a seat and tell me what brings you back?'

Alvarez sat.

'Would you prefer Señora Rowley to leave?' Heron asked, as he returned to the settee.

She spoke quickly. 'Whatever the inspector prefers, I'm staying.'

'But—'

'I'm staying.'

As Alvarez had judged, there was steel behind that friendly, warm manner. She would fight and go on fighting. 'Señor, I have no objection to the señora remaining, but perhaps it would be better for her not to do so.'

'Does no one understand English?' she snapped.

'Very well. Señor, as I have told you, two empty cartridge cases were found outside the front door of this house. I asked if you knew where they had come from and you replied you did not. I now need to ask you again. Whilst living here, have you been in possession of a Colt automatic?'

'No.'

Hilary reached out to hold his hand.

'Have you ever been in possession of cartridges which would fit a point three eight Colt automatic?'

'No.'

'You would like to consider your answer?'

'Why? That is the truth.'

'I fear not.'

'When I say—'

'Your fingerprints were on the empty cartridge cases found in the flowerbed.'

There was a long silence. Hilary gripped Heron's hand more tightly. He stared at Alvarez, past him, back at him and then away.

'One thing is certain, señor, you had both those cases in your hand.'

'I forgot when you first asked me. And having said what I did—'

'You forgot what?'

'I was so shocked.'

'Can't you begin to understand the terrible state he was in?' Hilary demanded, her voice high.

'I have to have an explanation, señora.'

Heron said, 'I walked into the bedroom, saw her, hurried forward . . . I didn't, couldn't see where I was going and trod on one of the cases, slipped and all but fell. I don't know why, but I picked that up with the other one. Later, when I was downstairs, I threw them out of the house. It sounds stupid now, but I suppose it could have been a symbolic gesture of rejection of what I had seen.'

'Or you had done?'

'I've just told you—'

'Is almost certainly a lie. Please, señor, tell me the truth.'

'I have.'

'Had you trodden on one of the cases, you would have marked it and most probably indented it. Forensics would have recorded the fact. They didn't.'

'Maybe I didn't actually step on it, even though that's how it seemed; I merely touched it, but almost lost my balance in reaction.'

'Señor, I have been ordered to arrest you unless you can give me a feasible explanation for how your prints came to be on the cases.'

'No!' Hilary said violently.

'Señora, there is much evidence which inculpates the señor.'

'I don't care. He did not kill Belinda. Why won't you

truly understand what kind of a man he is? He wouldn't divorce her because he had sworn at the wedding to love and honour her until death parted them. He'd no love left because she offered none, but he still had to honour his honour. He took every precaution to prevent her learning about us because to do so would shock and hurt her. Avoiding that was more important than anything. He's from the past, when one's word was one's bond, when one worried about other people before oneself.

'Please, please, try to understand him so that you will realize how impossible it is for him to have killed her.'

'Señora, had I not judged him to be the man you tell me he is, I would have arrested him before.'

'Then what's changed?'

'I have now been ordered to do so.'

'Why?'

'Forget it,' Heron said despairingly. 'If the inspector has his orders—'

'I must know why.'

'Señora, I will try to answer some of your questions. Señora Heron could not control the capital in her trust fund so even had she wanted to leave it to the señor, she could not. She left the house to one person, her jewellery to another, and only the residue of her estate to her husband. She had overlooked that the residue included the proceeds of her life insurance. The señor was all but disinherited unless the señora died before she could cancel the life insurance policy.'

'Is that supposed to have been his motive?'

'The sum involved provides a strong one.'

'Ten times that and he wouldn't have killed her.'

'He was seen to leave your house not long after eleven that night; he was returning in order to collect his wife whom, he thought, would be arriving at the airport much later. At ten past midnight, a shot was heard coming from the direction of the house. The señor reported the death of his wife roughly an hour after he had returned home. One would have expected him to do so immediately.

'During my investigation, I have repeatedly asked him if

he was in possession of a gun and cartridges and he has repeatedly denied this. Yet an automatic was seen in a drawer in his dressing room. The señora was shot twice. Two empty cartridge cases have been found and on them are his fingerprints.'

'He's explained what happened.'

'I fear his explanation is not easily accepted.'

'He told me that . . . that when she died, the gun had been pressed against her head.'

'For the second shot, that is so.'

'And you think . . . you think he could shoot her like some beastly hired assassin, yet wouldn't divorce her because of his promise in church? It doesn't matter what you've said, you don't begin to know people. And can't be bothered to try to.'

'Steady,' Heron said softly.

'I won't be quiet. He claimed he understood what kind of a person you are. He understands nothing. He's determined to arrest you and we can't do anything. It's like when I was married to Stanley. For week after week, I had to watch him slowly, agonizingly leave me. I begged the doctor to end his agony, he wouldn't. I prayed. Useless because, as I was forced to learn, there was no one listening. He died and my world collapsed. Then I met you and the world came alive once more. Now, it's happening all over again. It's hopeless . . .' She began to cry, covered her face with her hands.

When Alvarez saw mental pain in another, he suffered himself. He struggled to offer some relief, said, 'I am trying to prove the señor is innocent, señora.'

She uncovered her face, streaked with tears. 'By accusing him of murdering Belinda?'

Later, Alvarez blamed temporary madness, occasioned by her hopeless grief, for what he next said. 'Señora, from the beginning, I refused to believe the señor guilty. I judged him to be the man you tell me he is. Every time I learned a fact which pointed to his guilt, I tried to fault it and failed. When his prints were found on the cases, I did wonder if I had been fooling myself. But then I told myself that the truth of character cannot be faked, only obscured, and there was no obfuscation.'

'If you believe him innocent, why are you here?'

'I was ordered by my superior, who is convinced the señor is guilty; he does not believe character can negate evidence.'

'Then you are about to arrest me?' Heron said dully.

'No!' she cried.

'Señora, you are correct,' Alvarez said. 'I cannot arrest a man whom I believe to be innocent.' His temporary madness increased. 'Equally, I cannot arrest a man who is not here, and since I need to drive to the port to fetch something, what can I do if on my return the señor is gone?'

Heron, his voice reflecting astonishment, said, 'You are suggesting I run for it?'

'I suppose one might think that.'

'Yet you are a detective.'

'Who has learned that there are times when justice needs to be diverted if it is to be just.'

'How does one run away on an island when every means of exit can rapidly be closed?'

'By not running. Tell the staff you are going to Menorca. Drive down to Port Playa Neuva and leave your car as near to the departure quay of the Menorquin ferry as you can. The señora will have followed in her car and you join her to drive to Santa Helena. It is a little village, high up in the heart of the mountains. Many years ago, villagers collected snow in the snow bunkers to take to the cities in the summer and made charcoal, but there was no farming except for sheep and goats. So they were poor. They remain a separate people. José Moll lives there. Tell him I would like him to look after you, as a shepherd looks after his sheep. He will know what to do.'

'If it is ever found out what you have done . . .'

'Best not to consider the possibility.'

Alvarez sat at his desk, a glass of brandy at the ready.

'Yes?' Salas demanded over the phone.

'I am sorry to ring you so late in the evening—'

'It would be more to the point if you were to tell me why you are calling.'

'I have visited Ca'n Ajo.'

'You arrested Heron?'

'No, señor.'

'You misunderstood my order? Impossible. So now you are about to give me an absurd and illiterate reason for ignoring it.'

'I don't think so.'

'You accept the impossibility of denying your incompetence?'

'I am saying I don't think the reason I am about to give shows incompetence. He wasn't at his home.'

'It naturally did not occur to you to wait there until he returned?'

'I had a word with the staff and they'd heard him say he was going to Menorca. I asked the Policia Local at Playa Neuva to check whether his car was near the ferry terminal and they reported that it is. It would seem that that is where he has gone.'

'Why?'

'I suppose he imagined he has a better chance of leaving unmarked from there than here where there would be a general watch at airport and ports for him.'

'I repeat the question. Why has he gone there?'

'If an alert is put out, the Menorquins will not move as rapidly and efficiently as we would—'

'He has gone there because your bumbling interrogations have warned him he is under deep suspicion and because you failed to arrest him the moment the evidence of his guilt was sufficient.'

'I still don't think—'

'I have neither the time nor the inclination to try to decipher your thoughts. Since you will not have alerted the authorities in Menorca—'

'I did so immediately, señor. I thought that more important than reporting to you first.'

Salas cut the connection.

*   *   *

Dolores studied Alvarez, who was half-heartedly eating a banana. 'Enrique, you must visit a doctor.'

'A psychiatrist would be more useful,' Jaime said and laughed.

Dolores ignored her husband. 'You have hardly spoken throughout the meal. You did not ask for a second helping even though it was a good *sopas*. You have refilled your glass only once. Are you in pain?'

'No.'

'Then what ails you? More trouble with that ridiculous Madrileño?'

'Not as yet.'

'Then what is the problem?'

'This and that.'

'This little blonde and that little brunette,' Jaime said.

She spoke angrily. 'You cannot understand that for once he has not made a fool of himself over some woman half his age? He is in trouble.'

'Maybe that's because she is.'

'If I am ever asked what is the greatest problem a marriage offers a woman, I will answer, a husband.'

'I was only trying to cheer things up.'

She stood as Alvarez dropped the banana skin on to his plate. 'Enrique, you will help me clear the table.' She walked through the bead curtain.

He collected up plates and glasses and put them on the tray. Jaime, surprised by his escape from having to help, hastily sat in front of the television after having switched it on.

Alvarez went through to the kitchen, placed the tray down on the table.

'Now, tell me what is wrong,' Dolores said quietly.

'It's just . . . is it ever justifiable to do wrong in order to do right? Can results ever justify means?'

'How can one answer without knowing what has happened?'

'I have broken the law.'

'Why?'

'To save an innocent man from prison and the woman he loves from losing him for many years.'

'If he is innocent, why should he fear prison?'

'The facts all appear to prove he murdered his wife.'

'You are talking about the Englishman?'

'Yes.'

'The facts are wrong?'

'Not necessarily wrong. But Salas, who scorns assumptions unless made by him, assumes Heron is guilty and has ordered his arrest. Señora Rowley, who is Heron's friend –' he noticed Dolores's lips tighten – 'his lover, was married to a man who died slowly and painfully and she has never forgotten the horror of her helplessness. Now she believes she must suffer again because I have been ordered to arrest Heron and the evidence is probably sufficient to bring a verdict of guilty.'

'If he did kill his wife—'

'He did not; could not. But knowing he would stand so little chance in court, I decided—' He stopped.

'What?'

'Better you don't know.'

'You are certain this Englishman is innocent?'

'As certain as one can be relying on instinct.'

'Your instincts are always good.'

'Salas would call them totally fallacious.'

'Like all his kind, he has no room for the heart. My mother used to say that a man who did wrong for the right reason was but a shadow of the man who did right for the wrong reason.'

It was probably the first time he had heard her mention one of her mother's sayings which did not castigate men.

Twenty-One

Alvarez parked in front of Ca'n Ajo. He crossed to the front door, stepped inside and called out.

Teresa appeared. 'Come back for another meal, have you?'

'I wish I could stay to enjoy what's on the menu, but I can't.'

'You want something else, then?'

'Yes, but unfortunately, none of you can give it to me.'

She looked curiously at him, said she'd work to do, left.

He made his way upstairs and into the señora's bedroom. In his mind, the body once more lay sprawled out on the floor and he shivered. For how long had she known what was about to happen? At such a moment, did the mind spin seconds into minutes, perhaps time infinite? Did it shout for help because the cavalry always turned up at the last moment? Except when the horses were at pasture and the troopers asleep.

He wondered why he had returned to the house. He had slept badly. He was proud of belonging to the Cuerpo, but had betrayed what it stood for. He had assured Dolores that his instinct had to be true, yet a sleepless night could find doubt in any faith. After breakfast, he had set off for the post, even though it was a Sunday and then something – instinct? – had caused him to turn aside, drive through the narrow, twisting streets of the village to Ca'n Ajo.

He walked to the window and stared out at the garden, not now imagining what it would be like if it were his, simply enjoying its fresh beauty. Nature had the power to soothe. It could not, though, recover the past.

He paced on one of the rugs, with its blaze of colour.

Suppose Heron had fooled him from the beginning? Could Heron have fooled Hilary as well, or was she a partner to his crime? Could a guilty party suffer such torment as she had appeared to endure when she had thought he was about to be arrested? Had it been false emotion? If she had accepted Heron as a murderer, could she have loved him as she so obviously did? Why not? Love knew no logic, accepted no boundaries, altered character.

He heard a phone ring. A moment later, Teresa shouted that he was wanted. He left the bedroom and went out on to the landing. 'What is it?'

'Someone English wanting the señora on the phone, but she can't speak Spanish.'

It would have been quicker to return to the bedroom, but he chose to go downstairs. He picked up the receiver. 'Good morning. Can I help you?'

'May I speak to Mrs Heron, please?'

'I am afraid not.'

'Oh . . . it is important.'

'I am Inspector Alvarez of the Cuerpo General de Policia.'

'You're a policeman?'

'That is so.'

'Has something happened to Mrs Heron?'

'I am afraid she is dead.'

'Good God!' A pause. 'Then it wasn't just hysteria . . .'

'Why do you say that, señorita?'

'Well, I mean . . . Presumably, it was suicide?'

He had never stepped on a live wire carrying several thousand volts, but now knew what it felt like.

'Wasn't it?' she asked.

'We think she was murdered.'

There was a brief pause. 'I think you should speak to Mr Jenner. Will you hold on, please?'

Concentrate on the unexplained and the inconsistencies. Why had he so quickly accepted, following Teresa's inability to answer his questions, that there was no point in pursuing the question of the phone calls which had so upset the señora when making them? Why had he not again questioned why Señora Heron, renowned for working her staff hard, had suddenly and without warning given them the evening off – the evening of her death?

'Jenner speaking. You are in Mallorca?'

'Yes, señor.'

'And Mrs Heron is dead and you believe she was murdered?'

'That is so.'

'Then . . .'

There was silence.

'Señor, will you explain why the lady to whom I was speaking thought Señora Heron might have committed suicide?'

'I'll try to explain. Mrs Heron came to England to consult me some months ago. That was because she believed – you will excuse her insular misconception – that she would gain better treatment here. She had certain internal problems. Various tests were carried out, the results of some of which were not available when she said she had to return home because her husband was having an affair with another woman and she was not going to leave him any longer to enjoy himself – we unwillingly learn unwanted details about our patients' private lives. I tried to persuade her to stay because treatment could start immediately if this proved necessary. She refused to do so.'

'What was her emotional state?'

'Best described as very disturbed. She was convinced she was suffering from cancer, as had her mother, who died in great distress. On more than one occasion, she said that if it was proved she had cancer, she would kill herself rather than suffer the pain and disabling effects of treatment. I tried to persuade her that success in treating the disease had markedly increased since her mother's death; that until the results of all the tests were known, it was premature to believe she was suffering from a malignant tumour. I failed. She insisted she would kill herself.'

'Was it cancer?'

'The tumour proved to be malignant. Even so, an operation and treatment would have had a good chance of success.'

'You told her the result of the tests?'

'My secretary will have done so.'

'When?'

'You need to ask her. I'll put you through. But before I do, is there anything more I can tell you?'

'I don't think so, señor.'

'Do you know who killed her and why?'

'Not yet. It has proved to be a very difficult case.'

'Shocking news . . . I'm putting you through.'

There was a brief pause, a couple of clicks, and the secretary said, 'Mr Jenner thinks I may be able to help you, Inspector?'

'Can you tell me if and when you phoned Señora Heron in Mallorca to give her the results of the tests she had undergone?'

'She phoned here, twice.'

'On what date?'

'I'll check. Won't be a moment.'

One moment became four. 'It was Thursday, the seventeenth.'

'At what times?'

'I'm afraid I didn't note either down. However, the first was some time before the second, which was very late in the evening when I was just finishing some work that was too important to be left.'

'Why did she phone?'

'To demand the result of the tests. I said we hadn't received the reports yet. She became . . . well, hysterical, and said that meant she did have cancer. I tried to tell her it meant nothing of the sort, but she wouldn't listen. It was a priority case and the results came through before I left the office and I was wondering whether to tell her or leave it until the next day, when she rang the second time.'

'How did she react to what you told her?'

'She would not listen when I tried to repeat what Mr Jenner had said about there being a good chance she would overcome the trouble if she returned here for an operation. She was a very emotional woman.'

Only when her own interests were concerned. He thanked her, replaced the receiver.

Teresa called out from the end of the hall, 'Was it important?'

He had not noticed her standing there. 'Probably.'

'Isn't it your job to be certain?'

He smiled at her impudent question.

'So what are you going to do now?'

'Drive up to the mountains and enjoy their indifference to the problems of us humans.'

'You can talk very odd.'

Salas would agree with her.

Few tourists were aware, or cared, that in the heart of the island there was cold beauty. A holiday was not to be wasted on gazing at mountains whose crests wove strange patterns in the sky and whose rock faces were striated by that omnipotent destroyer, time. Far more rewarding to sunbathe too long, eat and drink too much, express contempt for anything unfamiliar.

Alvarez drove up into Santa Helena, perched on the side of a mountain, parked outside Ca'n Molet. It had been a frightening drive. Roads backed by unguarded drops of tens of metres; turns so acute that wheels came within millimetres of disaster; oncoming cars driven by lunatics; overtaking cars hooting their derision at his slowness. At one moment, he had even heard the Lorelei singing, to lure him to destruction.

'You look like you've just climbed out of your grave,' José Moll said, as Alvarez entered the *entrada* of the small, stone-built terrace house.

'Pour me a coñac; a large one.'

'You've had an accident?'

'It is shaking hands with death to drive here on roads that even a mule would refuse to walk.'

Moll laughed. 'Youngsters from the village think nothing of returning from their nightly pleasures doing sixty, seventy.'

'I am no longer young enough to be invulnerable.'

'Sit down and I'll bring the coñac – which is none of
the smart ones you drink down at the coast when the tourists
are buying. Memory tells me it's four fingers at least, and
only ice.'

Moll left the *entrada*, Alvarez sat. He had not been in
the house for quite a long time, but nothing had changed;
the framed family photographs still hung unevenly on the
walls, the chairs had not been cleaned, the aspidistra in a
brass pot seemed to be wilting under the dust. After a wife
died, a man could not find reason to keep the house as she
had.

Moll returned with two well-filled glasses. Alvarez drank
and gradually memories of that frightening drive ceased to
scare him. 'Where's the señor?'

'At the bar, teaching Gaspar to play poker, while Gaspar
teaches him to drink *hierbas*.'

'Have there been any troubles with the villagers?'

'When I said he was a friend?'

'No one's been up here asking after him?'

'No one is ever here, except a thirsty inspector.'

'How is he in himself?'

'Worried, uneasy, nervous. Needs exercise. I told him to
walk round the village two or three times to steady himself
up, but he didn't seem to understand.'

'Hardly surprising since you'll have spoken in
Mallorquin.'

'From the look of you, some walking might do you some
good.'

They heard footsteps just before Heron entered the
entrada. He faced Alvarez. 'Is Hilary all right?'

'Yes, señor. I phoned her to say I was coming to see you
and she begged me to bring her, but I had to refuse. She
said she'd phone you on the mobile. Again I had to deny
her the pleasure. One never knows what eyes are watching,
what ears are listening. She asked me to tell you, she sends
you everything you could wish.'

Heron stared into a private distance before he returned
to the small room. 'They still don't know I am here?'

'They are searching for you in Menorca.' Alvarez spoke to Moll in Mallorquin. 'Would you like to pour the señor a drink? And whilst you're about it, you can top up my glass.'

'You've no concern for your liver; if you still have one.' He collected Alvarez's glass, picked up his own, left.

Heron nervously asked, 'Why are you here? What's happened?'

'I have to learn the truth from you.'

'I've told you the truth, time and again.'

'Not once.'

'You're trying to say I did kill Belinda?'

'I am certain you did not, but I need you to explain what happened.'

'You believe me, yet I'm a liar?'

'There was a telephone call from England when I was at Ca'n Ajo. I answered it, to help your staff. Señor, did you know why your wife travelled to London in the middle of the month?'

'To see the trustees of the fund.'

Moll returned, handed out glasses. 'Are you going to do more talking?'

'I hope so,' Alvarez answered.

'There ain't no fun in listening to jabbering.' He walked out.

Alvarez drank, lowered his glass. 'You did not know your wife went there to consult a specialist in oncology?'

'She . . . she had cancer?'

'She feared she had and tests proved her fears to be justified, but she did not know this until she was back on the island. I have spoken to the specialist who saw her and he told me that she was hysterically afraid of the suffering cancer can involve; she had said that if the tests proved positive, she would commit suicide. He tried to reassure her, explained that an operation and further treatment should result in remission, but she would not listen.

'She was desperate to return home because in times of mental chaos, home can provide some comfort; she managed to board an earlier plane than the one she was due to take, reached home and learned from Riba, the private detective, final confirmation of your close friendship with Señora Rowley. She phoned London to ask if the results of the tests were known and learned that unfortunately they were positive. Then she gave Eva and Teresa the night off, saying she did not wish to eat. The two reports affected her so severely, she determined to carry out what she had threatened in London . . . She knew you possessed a gun and ammunition, so she loaded the gun in your dressing room, carried it into her bedroom.

'There was doubt and fear. She opened a bottle of champagne and drank quite heavily. She saw her suicide as a way of punishing you, knowing the guilt you would suffer, and that helped her overcome fear. But just before she shot herself, she found one last way to hurt you. She symbolically wrote "cancelled" across her life insurance policy, knowing her suicide would invalidate it and leave you with almost nothing.

'Now, señor, you will tell me – is that some of the truth?'

'It . . . it is the humiliating truth, though I knew nothing of her health problems.' He finished his brandy.

'Please tell me the rest.'

Time passed before he spoke in a low voice. 'After I met Hilary, life became golden. She lived rather quietly because her husband's death still distressed her and her income was not large. I had an income, but Belinda demanded I pay almost all of it towards the running of the house. So when I was free to live with Hilary, I wanted to provide her with things she had had to miss. I suppose . . . All right, I was hoping Belinda would die first. I knew I would inherit only the proceeds of the life insurance, but that would have made a welcome difference.

'One morning when we were eating breakfast, Belinda remarked she had asked a lawyer in London to check her will and make certain I inherited no more than her petty cash; he had replied in a letter she had just received. Since the life insurance was not specifically mentioned, the proceeds would pass to me. She smiled as she said that she couldn't let that happen or I'd have a happy old age.

'She flew to London and I spent my time with Hilary. That Thursday night, the front door was unlocked. I immediately thought we'd had another burglary and checked the house to see what was missing. I found her lying on the floor, dead, but . . . God knows why, I moved her until I could make certain there was no pulse.' He became silent.

Alvarez waited before he said, 'And then?'

'I realized –' he drew in a deep breath – 'she had committed suicide, which meant the life insurance was invalid. And so I . . .'

'You did what?'

'You want to strip my soul naked?'

'I want to hear the truth.'

'If the policy remained valid, I would inherit the two hundred and fifty thousand pounds. But how to conceal her suicide? I tried to find an answer and couldn't. I left and poured myself a very strong whisky, returned and suddenly found that answer. If her death appeared to be murder, the policy would be valid . . . Money twists the mind . . . I picked up the suicide note . . .'

'What had she written?'

'About her hatred of Hilary and me in foul terms, and she accused me of being responsible for her suicide.'

'You still have the note.'

'I tore it up. Only . . .'

'Yes?'

'I then picked up the bits.'

'Why?

'I don't know.'

'I think you do.'

'You have to know how warped a human mind can become? I thought that if I was ever about to be overcome by remorse, it would provide justification for what I was about to do.'

'Which was?'

'I picked up the gun and shot her, then moved the body back to how it had been before I checked her pulse.'

Facts could be construed so misleadingly. It had seemed

the first shot must have been badly aimed, had hit her thigh and brought her down, allowing the muzzle to be put against her head to make certain a second shot was fatal.

Heron picked up his glass, found it was empty, replaced it. 'What happens now?'

'Since she committed suicide, you cannot benefit from the insurance.'

'Having regained sanity, I couldn't take it.'

Alvarez admired the sentiment, wondered.

'Are you going to arrest me?'

'We need to examine the circumstances. You have been guilty of owning an unlicensed gun and ammunition. Reason for a fine, no more. You can be said to have tried to pervert the course of justice, but that almost always refers to an attempt to avoid criminal responsibility, not wrongly to introduce it. You shot a dead woman. Is that a crime? I confess, I do not know.

'Yet justice is an octopus – it meets a victim, wraps its tentacles around him and there is no escape. A lawyer would find reason for the law to take you to court.'

'And expose me for the callous bastard I was.'

'Probably, since no one would be able to understand you were not primarily thinking of yourself.'

'Then what happens?'

'We need another drink to stir our imaginations.' He called out in Mallorquin, 'José, do you always leave your guests to die of thirst?'

Back came the shout, 'If I were a hundred times richer, I could not afford to keep your glass filled.'

Alvarez held the receiver to his ear, tapped on the desk with the fingers of his right hand as he waited.

'Yes?' Salas said curtly.

'Good morning, señor. I am Inspector Alvarez from—'

'You have not read my new order? I have laid it down that inspectors are no longer to waste my time giving the comarques from which they speak.'

'That's interesting.'

'I do not require your judgment of the order.'

'Of course not, señor. But I was referring to your having used the word "comarques".'

'To find that interesting suggests a very restricted mind.'

'You don't understand.'

'To understand you is often a feat which strains human ability.'

'It is a Mallorquin word. You have always strongly decried the language, so it is surprising to hear you use it, especially as Madrileños usually won't speak anything but their kind of Castilian.'

'There is only one kind and that is Castilian spoken correctly, as in Madrid, not the degraded form one hears on this island. Have you any reason for speaking to me other than a desire to waste my time with more nonsensical comments?'

'I have a report to make on the Heron case.'

'Make it.'

'Señor Heron did not shoot and kill his wife. However, he did shoot her—'

'One expects any report from you to be incoherent, incomprehensible and inconsistent, but by denying and asserting the same fact in succeeding sentences, you excel yourself.'

'I was about to add that he shot her when she was dead.'

'You have been drinking?'

'I never drink when on duty.'

'You are under the influence of drugs?'

'Certainly not.'

'Then you will see the Cuerpo doctor and ask him to determine what mental disease you are suffering from.'

'Señor Heron returned home to find his wife dead in her bedroom. She had committed suicide—'

'And you are now going to tell me that having done so, she picked up the gun and two cartridge cases, went downstairs, threw the cases out of the front door, dropped the gun down the well, returned upstairs and lay down to confirm she was dead. Are there no limits to your fantasized imagination?'

'He was so shocked he did not think about what he was

doing. Instead of leaving everything as it was so the truth would immediately be visible, he started clearing up because his wife had a fetish about tidiness and in the strange way in which a very distressed mind works, he wanted the room to be perfectly tidy.'

'With her dead on the floor?'

'I did say his mind was very distressed. When he picked up the gun, he inadvertently pulled the trigger. The bullet struck his dead wife in the thigh. The further shock jerked his mind back to normal and he realized what the situation truly was. Now terrified he might be falsely accused of killing her, he got rid of the gun and the cartridge cases to make it seem someone had broken into the house and killed her. Of course, later, when calmer, he understood he had placed himself in a very dangerous situation, but by then it was too late to do anything. He just hoped the Cuerpo would uncover the truth.'

'Would not uncover it.'

'Why do you now say that, señor?'

'She was rich, he was having an affair, stood to gain by his wife's death—'

'No, señor.'

'I order you not to interrupt me.'

'I thought you would wish to understand that he inherits little since almost all she owned is left to other people.'

'Roughly four hundred thousand euros is almost nothing?'

'When she committed suicide, the policy became void.'

'Where is the proof it was suicide? Heron's word that it was? Where is the court who would believe him?'

'She left a suicide note. It was written in vicious terms and expressed her intention of killing herself. It was so virulent, Señor Heron tore it up, but was able to retrieve the bits and has given them to me.'

'Why the devil didn't you tell me that at the beginning? Have you had the note verified as genuine? You will write your report in full detail, you will provide corroboration for every statement, you will have that on my desk by tomorrow morning.'

The line went dead. Alvarez looked at his watch. Time

for a delayed *merienda*. The phone rang. He swore, picked up the receiver.

'How did you speak to him?' Salas demanded.

'To Señor Heron?'

'You imagine I am referring to the prime minister? Heron is in Menorca and I have received no request from you to travel there.'

'He never was in Menorca.'

'You told me he had fled there to escape justice.'

'He was cleverer than I.'

'Inevitably.'

'He told his staff he was going there, left his car down by the ferry berth, bought a ticket, but never sailed, reckoning we would not be searching for him on this island.'

'He made a complete fool of you.'

'I fear so.'

'Where has he been hiding?'

'He refuses to tell me in case I charge the owner. Yet, as I explained to him, unless the person concerned knew he was hiding from the police, there could be no reason to do so.'

'How did you know where he was?'

'I didn't and don't. He phoned me to arrange a meeting on neutral ground in order to tell me the truth.'

'Why did you not immediately inform me of that?'

'You would probably have ordered his arrest.'

'I had ordered it.'

'Yes, señor.'

'And you deliberately disobeyed the order, an offence which – I have little doubt – will be considered so serious, that following a report from me, the director general will consider your ill-starred career in the Cuerpo should be ended.'

'You will, of course, do whatever you consider to be right, señor, and that regardless of the consequences to yourself.'

'What is that supposed to mean?'

'When Señor Heron's innocence is proved beyond all doubt, it will become obvious you had ordered me to arrest an innocent man on insufficient and wrongly conceived evidence. I should not have thought you would wish that, considering the harm it could do to your future promotion.'

Salas shouted, 'The devil needs a bloody long spoon when he sups with you, Alvarez,' before he slammed down the receiver.